D0945973

Praise for FAMILY D.

"A genius for empathy . . . [Leavitt's] stories show great talent, and many a writer would be grateful to have written them."

—The New York Times Book Review

"He is in full command of a sharp, elegant style, and he already displays in these nine stories a knowledge of others' lives, their pains and losses, that a writer twice his age might envy."

—USA Today

"A first collection of unusual finesse. Leavitt has justly been praised for his deft handling of sensitive themes." *—Newsweek*

"A fine first appearance, the very sort of book that makes one imme- diately want more." *—Chicago Tribune*

"A most impressive entrance into contemporary fiction."

—Associated Press

"Leavitt has succeeded in balancing familiarity and insight. The stories are so recognizable that you'll want to read more to learn your own secrets." *—Vogue*

"Remarkably gifted." *—The Washington Post*

"Astonishing . . . David Leavitt is an extraordinary talent . . . This young writer shows promise of becoming one of what Virginia Woolf called the great truth-tellers. Every story in his collection is imme- diately gripping and completely believable."

—The Plain Dealer (Cleveland)

JUN   2018

"Luminous, touching and splendid. There isn't a one of them that isn't riveting and perceptive." —*The Sun* (Baltimore)

"Regardless of age, few writers so effortlessly achieve the sense of maturity and earned compassion evident in these stories . . . Mr. Leavitt's stories have the power to move us with the blush of truth" —*The New York Times*

"Brilliantly written." —*San Francisco Chronicle*

"An insightful portrait of people in turmoil." —*Los Angeles Times*

"America has a brand-new, sharp-witted observer in its midst . . . a perceptive, probing chronicler of our time . . . a skilled and artful storyteller who in the course of his writing is able to capture the textures and traumas of middle-class life." —*The Sacramento Bee*

Family Dancing

BY THE SAME AUTHOR

Novels

The Lost Language of Cranes
Equal Affections
While England Sleeps
The Page Turner
Martin Bauman; or, A Sure Thing
The Body of Jonah Boyd
The Indian Clerk
The Two Hotel Francforts

Stories and Novellas

A Place I've Never Been
Arkansas
The Marble Quilt
Collected Stories

Nonfiction

Italian Pleasures (with Mark Mitchell)
In Maremma: Life and a House in Southern Tuscany
(with Mark Mitchell)
Florence, A Delicate Case
*The Man Who Knew Too Much: Alan Turing
and the Invention of the Computer*

Family Dancing

Stories

DAVID LEAVITT

B L O O M S B U R Y

NEW YORK · LONDON · NEW DELHI · SYDNEY

For their contribution to the final shaping of these stories,
I would like to express my gratitude to Bobbie Bristol,
Mary D. Kierstead, and Andrew Wylie.

D.L.

Copyright © 1983, 1984 by David Leavitt

All rights reserved. No part of this book may be used or reproduced in any
manner whatsoever without written permission from the publisher except
in the case of brief quotations embodied in critical articles or reviews. For
information address Bloomsbury USA, 1385 Broadway, New York, NY 10018.

Published by Bloomsbury USA, New York

Bloomsbury is a trademark of Bloomsbury Publishing Plc

All papers used by Bloomsbury USA are natural, recyclable products made
from wood grown in well-managed forests. The manufacturing processes
conform to the environmental regulations of the country of origin.

LIBRARY OF CONGRESS CATALOGING-IN-PUBLICATION DATA HAS BEEN APPLIED FOR.

ISBN: 978-1-62040-704-2

"Territory" and "Out Here" originally appeared in slightly different form in *The New
Yorker*. "Counting Months" originally appeared in slightly different form in *Harper's*
and in *The O. Henry Awards: Prize Stories of 1984*. "Radiation" originally appeared
in slightly different form in *Prism* under the title "In the Radiation Center."

Family Dancing was first published by Knopf in 1984
and was included in *Collected Stories*, published by Bloomsbury in 2003
This U.S. edition published by Bloomsbury USA in 2014

1 3 5 7 9 10 8 6 4 2

Typeset by Hewer Text UK Ltd, Edinburgh
Printed and bound in the U.S.A. by Thomson-Shore Inc., Dexter, Michigan

Bloomsbury books may be purchased for business or promotional use. For
information on bulk purchases please contact Macmillan Corporate and
Premium Sales Department at specialmarkets@macmillan.com.

*For my mother
and for Debbie Keates*

. . . Though white is
the color of worship and of mourning, he

is not here to worship and he is too wise
to mourn—a life prisoner but reconciled.
With trunk tucked up compactly—the elephant's
sign of defeat—he resisted, but is the child

of reason now. His straight trunk seems to say: when
what we hoped for came to nothing, we revived.

Marianne Moore, "Elephants"

Contents

Territory   1

Counting Months   25

The Lost Cottage   50

Aliens   72

Danny in Transit   87

Family Dancing   109

Radiation   134

Out Here   144

Dedicated   163

Territory

Neil's mother, Mrs. Campbell, sits on her lawn chair behind a card table outside the food co-op. Every few minutes, as the sun shifts, she moves the chair and table several inches back so as to remain in the shade. It is a hundred degrees outside, and bright white. Each time someone goes in or out of the co-op a gust of air-conditioning flies out of the automatic doors, raising dust from the cement.

Neil stands just inside, poised over a water fountain, and watches her. She has on a sun hat, and a sweatshirt over her tennis dress; her legs are bare, and shiny with cocoa butter. In front of her, propped against the table, a sign proclaims: MOTHERS, FIGHT FOR YOUR CHILDREN'S RIGHTS—SUPPORT A NON-NUCLEAR FUTURE. Women dressed exactly like her pass by, notice the sign, listen to her brief spiel, finger pamphlets, sign petitions or don't sign petitions, never give money. Her weary eyes are masked by dark glasses. In the age of Reagan, she has declared, keeping up the causes of peace and justice is a futile, tiresome, and unrewarding effort; it is therefore an effort fit only for mothers to keep up. The sun bounces off the window glass through which Neil watches her. His own reflection lines up with her profile.

Later that afternoon, Neil spreads himself out alongside the pool and imagines he is being watched by the shirtless Chicano gardener. But the gardener, concentrating on his pruning, is neither seductive nor seducible. On the lawn, his mother's large Airedales—Abigail, Lucille, Fern—amble, sniff, urinate. Occasionally, they accost the gardener, who yells at them in Spanish.

After two years' absence, Neil reasons, he should feel nostalgia, regret, gladness upon returning home. He closes his eyes and tries to muster the proper background music for the cinematic scene of return. His rhapsody, however, is interrupted by the noises of his mother's trio—the scratchy cello, whining violin, stumbling piano—as she and Lillian Havalard and Charlotte Feder plunge through Mozart. The tune is cheery, in a Germanic sort of way, and utterly inappropriate to what Neil is trying to feel. Yet it *is* the music of his adolescence; they have played it for years, bent over the notes, their heads bobbing in silent time to the metronome.

It is getting darker. Every few minutes, he must move his towel so as to remain within the narrowing patch of sunlight. In four hours, Wayne, his lover of ten months and the only person he has ever imagined he could spend his life with, will be in this house, where no lover of his has ever set foot. The thought fills him with a sense of grand terror and curiosity. He stretches, tries to feel seductive, desirable. The gardener's shears whack at the ferns; the music above him rushes to a loud, premature conclusion. The women laugh and applaud themselves as they give up for the day. He hears Charlotte Feder's full nasal twang, the voice of a fat woman in a pink pants suit—odd, since she is a scrawny, arthritic old bird, rarely clad in anything other than tennis shorts and a blouse. Lillian is the fat woman in the pink pants suit; her voice is thin and warped by too much crying. Drink in hand, she calls out from the porch, "Hot enough!" and waves. He lifts himself up and nods to her.

The women sit on the porch and chatter; their voices blend with the clink of ice in glasses. They belong to a small circle of ladies all of whom, with the exception of Neil's mother, are widows and divorcées. Lillian's husband left her twenty-two years ago, and sends her a check every month to live on; Charlotte has been divorced twice as long as she was married, and has a daughter serving a long sentence for terrorist acts committed when she was nineteen. Only Neil's mother has a husband, a distant sort of husband, away often on business. He is away on business now. All of them feel betrayed—by husbands, by children, by history.

Neil closes his eyes, tries to hear the words only as sounds. Soon, a new noise accosts him: his mother arguing with the gardener in Spanish. He leans on his elbows and watches them; the syllables are loud, heated, and compressed, and seem on the verge of explosion. But the argument ends happily; they shake hands. The gardener collects his check and walks out the gate without so much as looking at Neil.

He does not know the gardener's name; as his mother has reminded him, he does not know most of what has gone on since he moved away. Her life has gone on, unaffected by his absence. He flinches at his own egoism, the egoism of sons.

"Neil! Did you call the airport to make sure the plane's coming in on time?"

"Yes," he shouts to her. "It is."

"Good. Well, I'll have dinner ready when you get back."

"Mom—"

"What?" The word comes out in a weary wail that is more of an answer than a question.

"What's wrong?" he says, forgetting his original question.

"Nothing's wrong," she declares in a tone that indicates that everything is wrong. "The dogs have to be fed, dinner has to be made, and I've got people here. Nothing's wrong."

"I hope things will be as comfortable as possible when Wayne gets here."

"Is that a request or a threat?"

"Mom—"

Behind her sunglasses, her eyes are inscrutable. "I'm tired," she says. "It's been a long day. I . . . I'm anxious to meet Wayne. I'm sure he'll be wonderful, and we'll all have a wonderful, wonderful time. I'm sorry. I'm just tired."

She heads up the stairs. He suddenly feels an urge to cover himself; his body embarrasses him, as it has in her presence since the day she saw him shirtless and said with delight, "Neil! You're growing hair under your arms !"

Before he can get up, the dogs gather round him and begin to sniff and lick at him. He wriggles to get away from them, but Abigail, the largest and stupidest, straddles his stomach and nuzzles his mouth. He splutters and, laughing, throws her off. "Get away from me, you goddamn dogs," he shouts, and swats at them. They are new dogs, not the dog of his childhood, not dogs he trusts.

He stands, and the dogs circle him, looking up at his face expectantly. He feels renewed terror at the thought that Wayne will be here so soon: Will they sleep in the same room? Will they make love? He has never had sex in his parents' house. How can he be expected to be a lover here, in this place of his childhood, of his earliest shame, in this household of mothers and dogs?

"Dinnertime! Abbylucyferny, Abbylucyferny, dinnertime!" His mother's litany disperses the dogs, and they run for the door.

"Do you realize," he shouts to her, "that no matter how much those dogs love you they'd probably kill you for the leg of lamb in the freezer?"

Neil was twelve the first time he recognized in himself something like sexuality. He was lying outside, on the grass, when Rasputin—the dog, long dead, of his childhood—began licking his face. He felt a tingle he did not recognize, pulled off his shirt to give the dog access to more of him. Rasputin's tongue tickled coolly. A wet nose started to sniff down his body, toward his bathing suit. What he felt frightened him, but he couldn't bring himself to push the dog away. Then his mother called out, "Dinner," and Rasputin was gone, more interested in food than in him.

It was the day after Rasputin was put to sleep, years later, that Neil finally stood in the kitchen, his back turned to his parents, and said, with unexpected ease, "I'm a homosexual." The words seemed insufficient, reductive. For years, he had believed his sexuality to be detachable from the essential him, but now he realized that it was part of him. He had the sudden, despairing sensation that though the words had been easy to say, the fact of their having been aired was incurably damning. Only then, for the first time, did he admit that they were true, and he shook and wept in regret for what he would not be for his mother, for having failed her. His father hung back, silent; he was absent for that moment as he was mostly absent—a strong absence. Neil always thought of him sitting on the edge of the bed in his underwear, captivated by something on television. He said, "It's O.K., Neil." But his mother was resolute; her lower lip didn't quaver. She had enormous reserves of strength to which she only gained access at moments like this one. She hugged him from behind, wrapped him in the childhood smells of perfume and brownies, and whispered, "It's O.K., honey." For once, her words seemed as inadequate as his. Neil felt himself shrunk to an

5

embarrassed adolescent, hating her sympathy, not wanting her to touch him. It was the way he would feel from then on whenever he was in her presence—even now, at twenty-three, bringing home his lover to meet her.

All through his childhood, she had packed only the most nutritious lunches, had served on the PTA, had volunteered at the children's library and at his school, had organized a successful campaign to ban a racist history textbook. The day after he told her, she located and got in touch with an organization called the Coalition of Parents of Lesbians and Gays. Within a year, she was president of it. On weekends, she and the other mothers drove their station wagons to San Francisco, set up their card tables in front of the Bulldog Baths, the Liberty Baths, passed out literature to men in leather and denim who were loath to admit they even had mothers. These men, who would habitually do violence to each other, were strangely cowed by the suburban ladies with their informational booklets, and bent their heads. Neil was a sophomore in college then, and lived in San Francisco. She brought him pamphlets detailing the dangers of bath-houses and back rooms, enemas and poppers, wordless sex in alleyways. His excursion into that world had been brief and lamentable, and was over. He winced at the thought that she knew all his sexual secrets, and vowed to move to the East Coast to escape her. It was not very different from the days when she had campaigned for a better playground, or tutored the Hispanic children in the audiovisual room. Those days, as well, he had run away from her concern. Even today, perched in front of the co-op, collecting signatures for nuclear disarmament, she was quintessentially a mother. And if the lot of mothers was to expect nothing in return, was the lot of sons to return nothing?

Driving across the Dumbarton Bridge on his way to the airport, Neil thinks, I have returned nothing; I have simply returned. He wonders if she would have given birth to him had she known what he would grow up to be.

Then he berates himself: Why should he assume himself to be the cause of her sorrow? She has told him that her life is full of secrets. She has changed since he left home—grown thinner, more rigid, harder to hug. She has given up baking, taken up tennis; her skin has browned and tightened. She is no longer the woman who hugged him and kissed him, who said, "As long as you're happy, that's all that's important to us."

The flats spread out around him; the bridge floats on purple and green silt, and spongy bay fill, not water at all. Only ten miles north, a whole city has been built on gunk dredged up from the bay.

He arrives at the airport ten minutes early, to discover that the plane has landed twenty minutes early. His first view of Wayne is from behind, by the baggage belt. Wayne looks as he always looks—slightly windblown—and is wearing the ratty leather jacket he was wearing the night they met. Neil sneaks up on him and puts his hands on his shoulders; when Wayne turns around, he looks relieved to see him.

They hug like brothers; only in the safety of Neil's mother's car do they dare to kiss. They recognize each other's smells, and grow comfortable again. "I never imagined I'd actually see you out here," Neil says, "but you're exactly the same here as there."

"It's only been a week."

They kiss again. Neil wants to go to a motel, but Wayne insists on being pragmatic. "We'll be there soon. Don't worry."

"We could go to one of the bathhouses in the city and take a room for a couple of aeons," Neil says. "Christ, I'm hard up. I don't even know if we're going to be in the same bedroom."

"Well, if we're not," Wayne says, "we'll sneak around. It'll be romantic."

They cling to each other for a few more minutes, until they realize that people are looking in the car window. Reluctantly, they pull apart. Neil reminds himself that he loves this man, that there is a reason for him to bring this man home.

He takes the scenic route on the way back. The car careers over foothills, through forests, along white four-lane highways high in the mountains. Wayne tells Neil that he sat next to a woman on the plane who was once Marilyn Monroe's psychiatrist's nurse. He slips his foot out of his shoe and nudges Neil's ankle, pulling Neil's sock down with his toe.

"I have to drive," Neil says. "I'm very glad you're here."

There is a comfort in the privacy of the car. They have a common fear of walking hand in hand, of publicly showing physical affection, even in the permissive West Seventies of New York—a fear that they have admitted only to one another. They slip through a pass between two hills, and are suddenly in residential Northern California, the land of expensive ranch-style houses.

As they pull into Neil's mother's driveway, the dogs run barking toward the car. When Wayne opens the door, they jump and lap at him, and he tries to close it again. "Don't worry. Abbylucyferny! Get in the house, damn it!"

His mother descends from the porch. She has changed into a blue flower-print dress, which Neil doesn't recognize. He gets out of the car and halfheartedly chastises the dogs. Crickets chirp in the trees. His mother looks radiant, even beautiful, illuminated by the headlights, surrounded by the now quiet dogs, like Circe with her slaves. When she walks over to Wayne, offering her hand, and says, "Wayne, I'm Barbara," Neil forgets that she is his mother.

"Good to meet you, Barbara," Wayne says, and reaches out his hand. Craftier than she, he whirls her around to kiss her cheek.

Barbara! He is calling his mother Barbara! Then he remembers that Wayne is five years older than he is. They chat by the open car door, and Neil shrinks back—the embarrassed adolescent, uncomfortable, unwanted.

So the dreaded moment passes and he might as well not have been there. At dinner, Wayne keeps the conversation smooth, like a captivated courtier seeking Neil's mother's hand. A faggot son's sodomist—such words spit into Neil's head. She has prepared tiny meatballs with fresh coriander, fettucine with pesto. Wayne talks about the street people in New York; El Salvador is a tragedy; if only Sadat had lived; Phyllis Schlafly—what can you do?

"It's a losing battle," she tells him. "Every day I'm out there with my card table, me and the other mothers, but I tell you, Wayne, it's a losing battle. Sometimes I think us old ladies are the only ones with enough patience to fight."

Occasionally, Neil says something, but his comments seem stupid and clumsy. Wayne continues to call her Barbara. No one under forty has ever called her Barbara as long as Neil can remember. They drink wine; he does not.

Now is the time for drastic action. He contemplates taking Wayne's hand, then checks himself. He has never done anything in her presence to indicate that the sexuality he confessed to five years ago was a reality and not an invention. Even now, he and Wayne might as well be friends, college roommates. Then Wayne, his savior, with a single, sweeping gesture, reaches for his hand, and clasps it, in the midst of a joke he is telling about Saudi Arabians. By the time he is laughing, their hands are joined. Neil's throat contracts; his heart begins to beat violently. He notices his mother's eyes flicker, glance downward; she never breaks the stride of her sentence. The dinner goes on, and every taboo nurtured since childhood falls quietly away.

She removes the dishes. Their hands grow sticky; he cannot tell which fingers are his and which Wayne's. She clears the rest of the table and rounds up the dogs.

"Well, boys, I'm very tired, and I've got a long day ahead of me tomorrow, so I think I'll hit the sack. There are extra towels for you in Neil's bathroom, Wayne. Sleep well."

"Good night, Barbara," Wayne calls out. "It's been wonderful meeting you."

They are alone. Now they can disentangle their hands.

"No problem about where we sleep, is there?"

"No," Neil says. "I just can't imagine sleeping with someone in this house."

His leg shakes violently. Wayne takes Neil's hand in a firm grasp and hauls him up.

Later that night, they lie outside, under redwood trees, listening to the hysteria of the crickets, the hum of the pool cleaning itself. Redwood leaves prick their skin. They fell in love in bars and apartments, and this is the first time that they have made love outdoors. Neil is not sure he has enjoyed the experience. He kept sensing eyes, imagined that the neighborhood cats were staring at them from behind a fence of brambles. He remembers he once hid in this spot when he and some of the children from the neighborhood were playing sardines, remembers the intoxication of small bodies packed together, the warm breath of suppressed laughter on his neck. "The loser had to go through the spanking machine," he tells Wayne.

"Did you lose often?"

"Most of the time. The spanking machine never really hurt—just a whirl of hands. If you moved fast enough, no one could actually get you. Sometimes, though, late in the afternoon, we'd get naughty. We'd chase each other and pull each other's pants down. That was all. Boys and girls together!"

"Listen to the insects," Wayne says, and closes his eyes.

Neil turns to examine Wayne's face, notices a single, small pimple. Their lovemaking usually begins in a wrestle, a struggle for dominance, and ends with a somewhat confusing loss of identity—as now, when Neil sees a foot on the grass, resting against his leg, and tries to determine if it is his own or Wayne's.

From inside the house, the dogs begin to bark. Their yelps grow into alarmed falsettos. Neil lifts himself up. "I wonder if they smell something," he says.

"Probably just us," says Wayne.

"My mother will wake up. She hates getting waked up."

Lights go on in the house; the door to the porch opens.

"What's wrong, Abby? What's wrong?" his mother's voice calls softly.

Wayne clamps his hand over Neil's mouth. "Don't say anything," he whispers.

"I can't just—" Neil begins to say, but Wayne's hand closes over his mouth again. He bites it, and Wayne starts laughing.

"What was that?" Her voice projects into the garden. "Hello?" she says.

The dogs yelp louder. "Abbylucyferny, it's O.K., it's O.K." Her voice is soft and panicked. "Is anyone there?" she asks loudly.

The brambles shake. She takes a flashlight, shines it around the garden. Wayne and Neil duck down; the light lands on them and hovers for a few seconds. Then it clicks off and they are in the dark—a new dark, a darker dark, which their eyes must readjust to.

"Let's go to bed, Abbylucyferny," she says gently. Neil and Wayne hear her pad into the house. The dogs whimper as they follow her, and the lights go off.

Once before, Neil and his mother had stared at each other in the glare of bright lights. Four years ago, they stood in the arena created by the headlights of her car, waiting for the train. He was on his way back to San Francisco, where he was marching in a Gay Pride Parade the next day. The train station was next door to the food co-op and shared its parking lot. The co-op, familiar and boring by day, took on a certain mystery in the night. Neil recognized the spot where he had skidded on his bicycle and broken his leg. Through the glass doors, the brightly lit interior of the store glowed, its rows and rows of cans and boxes forming their own horizon, each can illuminated so that even from outside Neil could read the labels. All that was missing was the ladies in tennis dresses and sweatshirts, pushing their carts past bins of nuts and dried fruits.

"Your train is late," his mother said. Her hair fell loosely on her shoulders, and her legs were tanned. Neil looked at her and tried to imagine her in labor with him—bucking and struggling with his birth. He felt then the strange, sexless love for women which through his whole adolescence he had mistaken for heterosexual desire.

A single bright light approached them; it preceded the low, haunting sound of the whistle. Neil kissed his mother, and waved goodbye as he ran to meet the train. It was an old train, with windows tinted a sort of horrible lemon-lime. It stopped only long enough for him to hoist himself on board, and then it was moving again. He hurried to a window, hoping to see her drive off, but the tint of the window made it possible for him to make out only vague patches of light—street lamps, cars, the co-op.

He sank into the hard, green seat. The train was almost entirely empty; the only other passenger was a dark-skinned man wearing bluejeans and a leather jacket. He sat directly across the aisle from Neil, next to the window. He had rough skin and a thick mustache. Neil discovered that by pretending to look out the window he could study the man's reflection in the lemon-lime glass. It was only slightly hazy—the quality of a bad photograph. Neil felt his mouth open, felt sleep closing in on him. Hazy red and gold flashes through

the glass pulsed in the face of the man in the window, giving the curi-
ous impression of muscle spasms. It took Neil a few minutes to realize that the man was staring at him, or, rather, staring at the back of
his head—staring at his staring. The man smiled as though to say, I
know exactly what you're staring at, and Neil felt the sickening
sensation of desire rise in his throat.

Right before they reached the city, the man stood up and sat down
in the seat next to Neil's. The man's thigh brushed deliberately against
his own. Neil's eyes were watering; he felt sick to his stomach. Taking
Neil's hand, the man said, "Why so nervous, honey? Relax."

Neil woke up the next morning with the taste of ashes in his mouth.
He was lying on the floor, without blankets or sheets or pillows.
Instinctively, he reached for his pants, and as he pulled them on came
face to face with the man from the train. His name was Luis; he turned
out to be a dog groomer. His apartment smelled of dog.

"Why such a hurry?" Luis said.

"The parade. The Gay Pride Parade. I'm meeting some friends to
march."

"I'll come with you," Luis said. "I think I'm too old for these
things, but why not?"

Neil did not want Luis to come with him, but he found it impossible to say so. Luis looked older by day, more likely to carry diseases.
He dressed again in a torn T-shirt, leather jacket, bluejeans. "It's my
everyday apparel," he said, and laughed. Neil buttoned his pants,
aware that they had been washed by his mother the day before. Luis
possessed the peculiar combination of hypermasculinity and effem-
inacy which exemplifies faggotry. Neil wanted to be rid of him, but
Luis's mark was on him, he could see that much. They would become
lovers whether Neil liked it or not.

They joined the parade midway. Neil hoped he wouldn't meet
anyone he knew; he did not want to have to explain Luis, who clung to

him. The parade was full of shirtless men with oiled, muscular shoulders. Neil's back ached. There were floats carrying garishly dressed prom queens and cheerleaders, some with beards, some actually looking like women. Luis said, "It makes me proud, makes me glad to be what I am." Neil supposed that by darting into the crowd ahead of him he might be able to lose Luis forever, but he found it difficult to let him go; the prospect of being alone seemed unbearable.

Neil was startled to see his mother watching the parade, holding up a sign. She was with the Coalition of Parents of Lesbians and Gays; they had posted a huge banner on the wall behind them proclaiming: OUR SONS AND DAUGHTERS, WE ARE PROUD OF YOU. She spotted him; she waved, and jumped up and down.

"Who's that woman?" Luis asked.

"My mother. I should go say hello to her."

"O.K.," Luis said. He followed Neil to the side of the parade. Neil kissed his mother. Luis took off his shirt, wiped his face with it, smiled.

"I'm glad you came," Neil said.

"I wouldn't have missed it, Neil. I wanted to show you I cared."

He smiled, and kissed her again. He showed no intention of introducing Luis, so Luis introduced himself.

"Hello, Luis," Mrs. Campbell said. Neil looked away. Luis shook her hand, and Neil wanted to warn his mother to wash it, warned himself to check with a V.D. clinic first thing Monday.

"Neil, this is Carmen Bologna, another one of the mothers," Mrs. Campbell said. She introduced him to a fat Italian woman with flushed cheeks, and hair arranged in the shape of a clamshell.

"Good to meet you, Neil, good to meet you," said Carmen Bologna. "You know my son, Michael? I'm so proud of Michael! He's doing so well now. I'm proud of him, proud to be his mother I am, and your mother's proud, too!"

The woman smiled at him, and Neil could think of nothing to say but "Thank you." He looked uncomfortably toward his mother, who stood listening to Luis. It occurred to him that the worst period of his life was probably about to begin and he had no way to stop it.

A group of drag queens ambled over to where the mothers were standing. "Michael! Michael!" shouted Carmen Bologna, and embraced a sticklike man wrapped in green satin. Michael's eyes were heavily dosed with green eyeshadow, and his lips were painted pink.

Neil turned and saw his mother staring, her mouth open. He marched over to where Luis was standing, and they moved back into the parade. He turned and waved to her. She waved back; he saw pain in her face, and then, briefly, regret. That day, he felt she would have traded him for any other son. Later, she said to him, "Carmen Bologna really was proud, and, speaking as a mother, let me tell you, you have to be brave to feel such pride."

Neil was never proud. It took him a year to dump Luis, another year to leave California. The sick taste of ashes was still in his mouth. On the plane, he envisioned his mother sitting alone in the dark, smoking. She did not leave his mind until he was circling New York, staring down at the dawn rising over Queens. The song playing in his earphones would remain hovering on the edges of his memory, always associated with her absence. After collecting his baggage, he took a bus into the city. Boys were selling newspapers in the middle of highways, through the windows of stopped cars. It was seven in the morning when he reached Manhattan. He stood for ten minutes on East Thirty-fourth Street, breathed the cold air, and felt bubbles rising in his blood.

Neil got a job as a paralegal—a temporary job, he told himself. When he met Wayne a year later, the sensations of that first morning returned to him. They'd been up all night, and at six they walked

15

across the park to Wayne's apartment with the nervous, deliberate gait of people aching to make love for the first time. Joggers ran by with their dogs. None of them knew what Wayne and he were about to do, and the secrecy excited him. His mother came to mind, and the song, and the whirling vision of Queens coming alive below him. His breath solidified into clouds, and he felt happier than he had ever felt before in his life.

The second day of Wayne's visit, he and Neil go with Mrs. Campbell to pick up the dogs at the dog parlor. The grooming establishment is decorated with pink ribbons and photographs of the owner's champion pit bulls. A fat, middle-aged woman appears from the back, leading the newly trimmed and fluffed Abigail, Lucille, and Fern by three leashes. The dogs struggle frantically when they see Neil's mother, tangling the woman up in their leashes. "Ladies, behave!" Mrs. Campbell commands, and collects the dogs. She gives Fern to Neil and Abigail to Wayne. In the car on the way back, Abigail begins pawing to get on Wayne's lap.

"Just push her off," Mrs. Campbell says. "She knows she's not supposed to do that."

"You never groomed Rasputin," Neil complains.

"Rasputin was a mutt."

"Rasputin was a beautiful dog, even if he did smell."

"Do you remember when you were a little kid, Neil, you used to make Rasputin dance with you? Once you tried to dress him up in one of my blouses."

"I don't remember that," Neil says.

"Yes. I remember," says Mrs. Campbell. "Then you tried to organize a dog beauty contest in the neighborhood. You wanted to have runners-up—everything."

"A dog beauty contest?" Wayne says.

"Mother, do we have to—"

16

"I think it's a mother's privilege to embarrass her son," Mrs. Campbell says, and smiles.

When they are about to pull into the driveway, Wayne starts screaming, and pushes Abigail off his lap. "Oh, my God!" he says. "The dog just pissed all over me."

Neil turns around and sees a puddle seeping into Wayne's slacks. He suppresses his laughter, and Mrs. Campbell hands him a rag.

"I'm sorry, Wayne," she says. "It goes with the territory."

"This is really disgusting," Wayne says, swatting at himself with the rag.

Neil keeps his eyes on his own reflection in the rearview mirror and smiles.

At home, while Wayne cleans himself in the bathroom, Neil watches his mother cook lunch—Japanese noodles in soup. "When you went off to college," she says, "I went to the grocery store. I was going to buy you ramen noodles, and I suddenly realized you weren't going to be around to eat them. I started crying right then, blubbering like an idiot."

Neil clenches his fists inside his pockets. She has a way of telling him little sad stories when he doesn't want to hear them—stories of dolls broken by her brothers, lunches stolen by neighborhood boys on the way to school. Now he has joined the ranks of male children who have made her cry.

"Mama, I'm sorry," he says.

She is bent over the noodles, which steam in her face. "I didn't want to say anything in front of Wayne, but I wish you had answered me last night. I was very frightened—and worried."

"I'm sorry," he says, but it's not convincing. His fingers prickle. He senses a great sorrow about to be born.

"I lead a quiet life," she says. "I don't want to be a disciplinarian. I just don't have the energy for these—shenanigans. Please don't frighten me that way again."

17

"If you were so upset, why didn't you say something?"

"I'd rather not discuss it. I lead a quiet life. I'm not used to getting woken up late at night. I'm not used—"

"To my having a lover?"

"No, I'm not used to having other people around, that's all. Wayne is charming. A wonderful young man."

"He likes you, too."

"I'm sure we'll get along fine."

She scoops the steaming noodles into ceramic bowls. Wayne returns, wearing shorts. His white, hairy legs are a shocking contrast to hers, which are brown and sleek.

"I'll wash those pants, Wayne," Mrs. Campbell says. "I have a special detergent that'll take out the stain."

She gives Neil a look to indicate that the subject should be dropped. He looks at Wayne, looks at his mother; his initial embarrassment gives way to a fierce pride—the arrogance of mastery. He is glad his mother knows that he is desired, glad it makes her flinch.

Later, he steps into the back yard; the gardener is back, whacking at the bushes with his shears. Neil walks by him in his bathing suit, imagining he is on parade.

That afternoon, he finds his mother's daily list on the kitchen table:

TUESDAY

7:00—breakfast
Take dogs to groomer
Groceries (?)

Campaign against Draft—4–7

Buy underwear
Trios—2:00
Spaghetti
Fruit
Asparagus if sale
Peanuts
Milk

Doctor's Appointment (make)
Write Cranston/Hayakawa
re disarmament

Handi-Wraps
Mozart
Abigail
Top Ramen
Pedro

Her desk and trash can are full of such lists; he remembers them from the earliest days of his childhood. He had learned to read from them. In his own life, too, there have been endless lists—covered with check marks and arrows, at least one item always spilling over onto the next day's agenda. From September to November, "Buy plane ticket for Christmas" floated from list to list to list.

The last item puzzles him: Pedro. Pedro must be the gardener. He observes the accretion of names, the arbitrary specifics that give a sense of his mother's life. He could make a list of his own selves: the child, the adolescent, the promiscuous faggot son, and finally the good son, settled, relatively successful. But the divisions wouldn't work; he is today and will always be the child being licked by the dog, the boy on the floor with Luis; he will still be everything he is ashamed of. The other lists—the lists of things done and undone—tell their own truth: that his life is measured more properly in objects than in stages. He knows himself as "jump rope," "book," "sunglasses," "underwear."

"Tell me about your family, Wayne," Mrs. Campbell says that night, as they drive toward town. They are going to see an Esther Williams movie at the local revival house: an underwater musical, populated by mermaids, underwater Rockettes.

"My father was a lawyer," Wayne says. "He had an office in Queens, with a neon sign. I think he's probably the only lawyer in the world who had a neon sign. Anyway, he died when I was ten. My mother never remarried. She lives in Queens. Her great claim to fame is that when she was twenty-two she went on 'The $64,000 Question.' Her category was mystery novels. She made it to sixteen thousand before she got tripped up."

"When I was about ten, I wanted you to go on 'Jeopardy,' " Neil says to his mother. "You really should have, you know. You would have won."

"You certainly loved 'Jeopardy,' " Mrs. Campbell says. "You used to watch it during dinner. Wayne, does your mother work?"

"No," he says. "She lives off investments."

"You're both only children," Mrs. Campbell says. Neil wonders if she is ruminating on the possible connection between that coincidence and their "alternative life style."

The movie theater is nearly empty. Neil sits between Wayne and his mother. There are pillows on the floor at the front of the theater, and a cat is prowling over them. It casts a monstrous shadow every now and then on the screen, disturbing the sedative effect of water ballet. Like a teenager, Neil cautiously reaches his arm around Wayne's shoulder. Wayne takes his hand immediately. Next to them, Neil's mother breathes in, out, in, out. Neil timorously moves his other arm and lifts it behind his mother's neck. He does not look at her, but he can tell from her breathing that she senses what he is doing. Slowly, carefully, he lets his hand drop on her shoulder; it twitches spasmodically, and he jumps, as if he had received an electric shock. His mother's quiet breathing is broken by a gasp; even Wayne notices. A sudden brightness on the screen illuminates the panic in her eyes, Neil's arm frozen above her, about to fall again. Slowly, he lowers his arm until his fingertips touch her skin, the fabric of her dress. He has gone too far to go back now; they are all too far.

Wayne and Mrs. Campbell sink into their seats, but Neil remains stiff, holding up his arms, which rest on nothing. The movie ends, and they go on sitting just like that.

"I'm old," Mrs. Campbell says later, as they drive back home. "I remember when those films were new. Your father and I went to one on our first date. I loved them, because I could pretend that those women underwater were flying—they were so graceful. They really took advantage of Technicolor in those days. Color was something to appreciate. You can't know what it was like to see a color movie for the first time, after years of black-and-white. It's like trying to explain the surprise of snow to an East Coaster. Very little is new anymore, I fear."

Neil would like to tell her about his own nostalgia, but how can he explain that all of it revolves around her? The idea of her life before he was born pleases him. "Tell Wayne how you used to look like Esther Williams," he asks her.

She blushes. "I was told I looked like Esther Williams, but really more like Gene Tierney," she says. "Not beautiful, but interesting. I like to think I had a certain magnetism."

"You still do," Wayne says, and instantly recognizes the wrongness of his comment. Silence and a nervous laugh indicate that he has not yet mastered the family vocabulary.

When they get home, the night is once again full of the sound of crickets. Mrs. Campbell picks up a flashlight and calls the dogs. "Abbylucyferny, Abbylucyferny," she shouts, and the dogs amble from their various corners. She pushes them out the door to the back yard and follows them. Neil follows her. Wayne follows Neil, but hovers on the porch. Neil walks behind her as she tramps through the garden. She holds out her flashlight, and snails slide from behind bushes, from under rocks, to where she stands. When the snails become visible, she crushes them underfoot. They make a wet, cracking noise, like eggs being broken.

"Nights like this," she says, "I think of children without pants on, in hot South American countries. I have nightmares about tanks rolling down our street."

"The weather's never like this in New York," Neil says. "When it's hot, it's humid and sticky. You don't want to go outdoors."

"I could never live anywhere else but here. I think I'd die. I'm too used to the climate."

"Don't be silly."

"No, I mean it," she says. "I have adjusted too well to the weather."

The dogs bark and howl by the fence. "A cat, I suspect," she says. She aims her flashlight at a rock, and more snails emerge—uncountable numbers, too stupid to have learned not to trust light.

"I know what you were doing at the movie," she says.

"What?"

"I know what you were doing."

"What? I put my arm around you."

"I'm sorry, Neil," she says. "I can only take so much. Just so much."

"What do you mean?" he says. "I was only trying to show affection."

"Oh, affection—I know about affection."

22

He looks up at the porch, sees Wayne moving toward the door, trying not to listen.

"What do you mean?" Neil says to her.

She puts down the flashlight and wraps her arms around herself. "I remember when you were a little boy," she says. "I remember, and I have to stop remembering. I wanted you to grow up happy. And I'm very tolerant, very understanding. But I can only take so much."

His heart seems to have risen into his throat. "Mother," he says, "I think you know my life isn't your fault. But for God's sake, don't say that your life is my fault."

"It's not a question of fault," she says. She extracts a Kleenex from her pocket and blows her nose. "I'm sorry, Neil. I guess I'm just an old woman with too much on her mind and not enough to do." She laughs halfheartedly. "Don't worry. Don't say anything," she says. "Abbylucyferny, Abbylucyferny, time for bed!"

He watches her as she walks toward the porch, silent and regal. There is the pad of feet, the clinking of dog tags as the dogs run for the house.

He was twelve the first time she saw him march in a parade. He played the tuba, and as his elementary-school band lumbered down the streets of their then small town she stood on the sidelines and waved. Afterward, she had taken him out for ice cream. He spilled some on his red uniform, and she swiped at it with a napkin. She had been there for him that day, as well as years later, at that more memorable parade; she had been there for him every day.

Somewhere over Iowa, a week later, Neil remembers this scene, remembers other days, when he would find her sitting in the dark, crying. She had to take time out of her own private sorrow to appease his anxiety. "It was part of it," she told him later. "Part of being a mother."

"The scariest thing in the world is the thought that you could unknowingly ruin someone's life," Neil tells Wayne. "Or even change someone's life. I hate the thought of having such control. I'd make a rotten mother."

"You're crazy," Wayne says. "You have this great mother, and all you do is complain. I know people whose mothers have disowned them."

"Guilt goes with the territory," Neil says.

"Why?" Wayne asks, perfectly seriously.

Neil doesn't answer. He lies back in his seat, closes his eyes, imagines he grew up in a house in the mountains of Colorado, surrounded by snow—endless white snow on hills. No flat places, and no trees; just white hills. Every time he has flown away, she has come into his mind, usually sitting alone in the dark, smoking. Today she is outside at dusk, skimming leaves from the pool.

"I want to get a dog," Neil says.

Wayne laughs. "In the city? It'd suffocate."

The hum of the airplane is druglike, dazing. "I want to stay with you a long time," Neil says.

"I know." Imperceptibly, Wayne takes his hand.

"It's very hot there in the summer, too. You know, I'm not thinking about my mother now."

"It's O.K."

For a moment, Neil wonders what the stewardess or the old woman on the way to the bathroom will think, but then he laughs and relaxes.

Later, the plane makes a slow circle over New York City, and on it two men hold hands, eyes closed, and breathe in unison.

Counting Months

M rs. Harrington was sitting in the oncology department waiting room and thinking about chicken when the realization came over her. It was like a fist knocking the wind out of her, making her need to gasp and whoop air. Suddenly the waiting room was sucking up and churning; the nurses, the magazine racks, the other patients turning over and over again like laundry in a washer. Faces grew huge, then shrank back away from her until they were unrecognizable. Dimly she felt the magazine she had been reading slip out of her hand and onto the floor.

Then it was over.

"Ma'am?" the woman next to her was asking. "Ma'am, are you all right?" she was asking, holding up the magazine Mrs. Harrington had dropped. It was *Family Circle*. "You dropped this," the woman said.

"Thank you," said Mrs. Harrington. She took the magazine. She walked over to the fish tank and dropped herself onto a soft bench. The fish tank was built into a wall that separated two waiting rooms and could be looked into from either side. Pregnant guppies, their egg sacs visible through translucent skin, were swimming in circles against the silhouette of a face, vastly distorted, that peered in from the other waiting room. One angelfish remained still, near the bottom, near the plastic diver in the corner.

Mrs. Harrington's breath was fogging the fish tank.

The thought had come to her the way the carrier of a plague comes to an innocent town. She was reading a Shake 'n' Bake ad, thinking about the chicken waiting to be cooked in the refrigerator at home, and whether she would broil it; she was tense. She began to consider the date, December 17th: Who was born on December 17th? Did anything historic happen on December 17th?

Then, through some untraceable process, that date—December 17th—infected her with all the horror of memory and death. For today was the day she was supposed to be dead by.

Mrs. Harrington?" she heard the head nurse call.

"Yes," she said. She got up and moved toward the long hallway along which the doctors kept their secret offices, their examination rooms. She moved with a new fear of the instruments she could glimpse through slightly open doors.

It was an intern who had told her, "Six months."

Then Dr. Sanchez had stood in front of her with his greater experience and said, "That's youthful hubris. Of course, we can't date these things. We're going to do everything we can for you, Anna. We're going to do everything humanly possible. You could live a long time, a full life."

But she had marked the date on a mental calendar: six months. December 17th would be six months. And so it was. And here she was, still alive, having almost forgotten she was to die.

She undressed quickly, put on the white paper examination gown, lay down on the cold table. Everything is the same, she told herself. Broil the chicken. Chicken for dinner. The Lauranses' party tonight. Everything is the same.

Then the horror swept through her again. Six months ago she had been planning to be dead by this day. Her children on their way to a new home. But it had been a long time.

Things dragged on. Radiation therapy, soon chemotherapy, all legitimate means of postponement. She lost quite a bit of hair, but a helpful lady at the radiation therapy center directed her to a hairdresser who specialized in such cases as hers, could cut around the loss and make it imperceptible. Things dragged on. She made dinner for her children.

She went to one meeting of a therapy group, and they told her to scream out her aggression and to beat a pillow with a hammer. She didn't go back.

"Hello, Anna," Dr. Sanchez said, coming in, sitting at the opposite end of the table. He smelled of crushed cigars, leather. "How're things?"

He obviously didn't remember. December 17th.

"Fine," she said.

As if she didn't notice, he began to feel around her thighs for lumps.

"The kids?" he said.

"Fine," she said.

"You've been feeling all right, I hear," he said.

"Fine," she said.

"And you aren't finding the results of the radiation too trying?"

"No, not bad."

"Well, I've got to be honest with you, when you start the chemotherapy in January, you're not going to feel so hot. You'll probably lose quite a bit of weight, and more hair. Feel like you have a bad flu for a while."

"I could stand to lose a few pounds," Mrs. Harrington said.

"Well, what's this?" said Dr. Sanchez, his hand closing around a new lump.

"You know, they come and go," said Mrs. Harrington, turning over. "That one on my back is pretty much gone now."

"Um-hum," said Dr. Sanchez, pressing between her buttocks. "And have you had any pain from the one that was pressing on the kidney?"

"No."

"That's good, very good."

He went on in silence. Every now and then he gave grunts of approval, but Mrs. Harrington had long since realized that rather than indicating some improvement in her condition, these noises simply signified that the disease was following the course he had mapped out for it. She lay there. It no longer embarrassed her, because he knew every inch of her body. Though there were certain things she had to be sure of before she went. She always made sure she was clean everywhere.

"Well," Dr. Sanchez said, pulling off his plastic gloves and throwing them into a repository, "you seem to be doing fine, Anna."

Fine. What did that mean? That the disease was fine, or her?

"I guess I just keep on, don't I?" she said.

"Seriously, Anna, I think it's marvellous the way you're handling this thing. I've had patients who've just given up to depression. A lot of them end up in hospitals. But you keep up an active life. Still on the PTA? Still entering cooking contests? I'll never forget those terrific brownies you brought. The nurses were talking about them for a week."

"Thank you, Doctor," she said. He didn't know. No more than the woman hitting the pillow with the hammer. All these months she had been so "active," she suddenly knew for a lie. You had to lie to live through death, or else you die through what's left of your life.

As she got dressed she wondered if she'd ever be able to sleep again, or if it would be as it was at the beginning, when she would go to sleep in fear of never waking up, and wake up unsure if she were really alive.

Lying there, terrified, in her flannel nightgown, the mouthpiece firmly in place (to prevent teeth-grinding), her eyes searching the ceiling for familiar cracks, her hands pinching what flesh they could find, as if pain could prove life.

It had taken her many months to learn to fall asleep easily again.

She was one with the people in the lobby now. She had been aloof from them before. One she knew, Libby, a phone operator. She waved from across the waiting room. Then there was the man with the bandage around his head. A younger woman, probably a daughter, always had to bring him. She noticed an older man with a goiter on his neck, or something that looked like a goiter, in the corner, looking at a fish.

"Good night," she said to the nurses, tying her scarf around her head. Paper Santa Clauses were pasted to the walls; a tiny tree gleamed dully in a corner. Outside the waiting room, the hospital corridors extended dim and yellow all the way to the revolving door. Mrs. Harrington pushed at the glass, and the first gusts of wind rose up, seeping in from outside. She pushed the glass away, emerging, thankfully, outside, and the cold, heavy wind seemed to bruise her alive again, brushing away the coat of exhaustion that had gathered on her eyelids while she was inside. It was cold, very cold. Her small heels crushed frozen puddles underfoot, so that they fragmented into tiny crystal mirrors. Rain drizzled down. California winter. She smoothed her scarf under her chin and walked briskly toward her car, a tall, thick woman, a genteel yacht in a harbor.

The car was cold. She turned on the heat and the radio. The familiar voice of the local newscaster droned into the upholstered interior, permeated it like the thick, unnatural heat. Rain clicked against the roof. Slowly she was escaping the hospital, merging into regular traffic. She saw the stores lit up, late-afternoon shoppers rushing home to dinner. She wanted to be one of them, to push a cart down the aisles of a supermarket again. She pulled into the Lucky parking lot.

In the supermarket the air was cool and fresh, smelled of peat and wet sod and lettuce. Small, high voices chirped through the public address system:

> *Our cheeks are red and rosy,*
> *and comfy cozy are we;*
> *We're snuggled up together*
> *like birds of a feather should be.*

Mrs. Harrington was amazed by the variety of brightly colored foods and packages, as if she had never noticed them before. She felt among the apples until she found one hard enough to indicate freshness; she examined lettuce heads. She bought SpaghettiOs for her youngest son, gravy mix, Sugar Pops. A young family pushed a cart past her, exuberant, the baby propped happily in the little seat at the top of the shopping cart, his bottom on red plastic and his tiny legs extending through the metal slats. She was forgetting.

An old woman stood ahead of her in the nine-items-or-less line. She was wearing a man's torn peacoat. She bought a bag of hard candy with seventy-eight cents in pennies, then moved out the electric doors. "We get some weird ones," the checkout boy told Mrs. Harrington. He had red hair and bad acne and reminded her of her oldest son.

*   *   *

Back in the car, she told herself, "Try to forget. Things aren't any different than they were yesterday. You were happy yesterday. You weren't thinking about it yesterday. You're not any different." But she was. The difference was growing inside her, through the lymph nodes, exploring her body.

It was all inside. At the group therapy session a woman had said, "I think of the cancer as being too alive. The body just keeps multiplying until it can't control itself. So instead of some dark interior alien growth that's killing me, it's that I'm dying of being too alive, of having lived too much. Isn't that better?" the woman had said, and everyone had nodded.

Or is it, Mrs. Harrington was thinking, the body killing itself, from within?

She was at a red light. "If the light changes by the time I count to five," she said, "I will become normal again. One. Two. Three. Four. Five."

It changed.

And maybe if I had asked for six, Mrs. Harrington was thinking, that would have meant another ten years. Ten years!

As soon as Mrs. Harrington got home, she hurried into the kitchen. Her son Roy was watching "Speed Racer" on television. He was fourteen. She heard loud music in the background: Jennifer; Blondie— "Dreaming, dreaming is free." And then the sounds of her youngest child, Ernest, imitating an airplane. She was grateful for the noise, for the chance to quiet them with her arrival.

"What's for dinner?" Roy asked.

"Nothing," Mrs. Harrington answered, "unless Jennifer cleans up like she promised. Jennifer!"

"Ma," Ernest said, flying into the kitchen, "the party's tonight, right? Timmy's gonna be there, right?"

"Right," she said. He was her youngest child. His nose was plugged with cotton because it had been bleeding.

Her daughter came in, sucking a Starburst. She had on a pink blouse Mrs. Harrington didn't much care for. "How was it?" she asked, beginning to scrub the pots.

"Fine," said Mrs. Harrington.

"What's for dinner?" Roy asked again.

"Chicken. Broiled chicken."

"Again?"

"Yes," Mrs. Harrington said, remembering the days before when chicken hadn't mattered. Those days took on a new luxury, a warmth to match Christmas, in this light—the four of them, eating, innocent.

"Can I make some noodles?" Roy asked.

"Noodles!" Ernest shouted.

"As long as *you* make them," Jennifer said.

Roy stuck out his chest in a mimicking gesture.

"I'll make them, I'll make them. In a few minutes," he said.

The boys left the room.

"Dad called," Jennifer said.

"Was he at home?"

"He and Sandy are in Missoula, Montana."

"Ha," said Mrs. Harrington. "One minute in Trinidad, the next in Missoula, Montana."

"He asked how you were."

"And what did you tell him?"

"The truth," said Jennifer.

"And what might that be?" asked Mrs. Harrington.

"Fine."

"Oh." Mrs. Harrington melted butter in a saucepan, for basting.

"Are you looking forward to the party tonight?" Mrs. Harrington asked.

"Yes," Jennifer said. "As long as there are some kids my age."

Occasional moments it came back to her, and she had to hold on to keep from fainting. Such as when she was sitting on the toilet, in her green bathrobe, among the plants, her panty hose and underpants around her knees. Suddenly the horror swept through her again, because in the last six months the simple act of defecation had been so severely obstructed by the disease—something pushing against the intestine.

She held the edges of the toilet with her hands. Pushed. She tried to imagine she was caught in ice, frozen, surrounded by glacial cold, and inside, only numb.

But then, looking at the bathroom cabinet—the rows of pills, the box with the enema, the mouthpiece to keep her from grinding her teeth (fit into her mouth like a handkerchief stuffed in there by a rapist)—it came back to her, all of it.

Roy tossed the noodles with butter and cheese; Jennifer sliced the chicken. A smell of things roasting, rich with herbs, warmed the kitchen.

"Niffer, is there more cheese?"

"Check the pantry."

"I'd get it if I could reach," Ernest said.

Their mother came in. "Looks like you've got everything under control," she said.

"I put paprika on the chicken," Jennifer said.

"I helped with dessert," Ernest said.

"It's true, he helped me operate the blender."

Mrs. Harrington set the table, laid out familiar pieces of stainless steel. One plate was chipped.

"Rat tart!" Roy was shrieking in a high imitation of a feminine voice. He was recounting something he had seen on television to his sister. She was laughing as she tossed salad. Ernest rolled on the floor, gasping, as if he were being tickled. Mrs. Harrington smiled.

They sat down to dinner.

Food made its way around the table—the bowl of noodles, the chicken, the salad. Everyone ate silently for a few minutes, in huge mouthfuls. "Eat more slowly," Mrs. Harrington said.

She wondered where they'd be today if, indeed, she had died. After all, in those frantic first weeks, she had planned for that possibility. Jennifer and Roy, she knew, were old enough to take care of themselves. But her heart went out to Ernest, who had stayed at her breast the longest, born late in life, born after the divorce had come through. Little Ernest—he had lots of colds, and few friends; crybaby, tattletale, once, a teacher told her, even a thief. He sat there across from her, innocent, a noodle hanging from his mouth.

"I wonder if Greg Laurans will be at the party," Jennifer said.

"Why, do you like him?" asked Roy, leering.

"Screw you. He's very involved." Jennifer reached to put a chicken liver she had accidentally taken back on the platter. "He runs a singing group at the state hospital through Young Life."

"Watch out for him, Jennifer," Mrs. Harrington said. "This is just another phase for him. Last year he was stealing cars."

"But he's been born again!" Ernest said loudly. He said everything loudly.

"Talk softer."

"He's reformed," Jennifer said. "But anyway, he won't be there. His parents aren't speaking to him, Gail told me."

Mrs. Harrington didn't blame the Lauranses. They were good Jews—gave a sizeable chunk of their income to the UJA. Jennifer played loud music and got low grades; Roy had bad acne, didn't wash enough, smoked a lot of marijuana; but compared to Greg Laurans, they were solid, loving kids, who knew what they wanted and weren't caught up in the craziness of the world.

Jennifer and Roy both knew about the illness—though of course she couldn't tell them "six months," and they never talked about time. She guessed, however, that they guessed what she guessed. Dr. Sanchez had told her, "If you're alive in two years, it won't be a miracle, but if you're not, we can't say it would be unexpected."

Ernest, however, knew nothing. He wasn't old enough. He wouldn't be able to understand. It would be hard enough for him, she had reasoned, after she was gone; at least let him live while he could under the pleasant delusion that she would be there for him forever.

But now, Mrs. Harrington stared across the table at her son, and the reasoning that had kept her going for six months seemed warped, perverse. The way it stood, she would die, for him, as a complete surprise. It might ruin him. He might turn into Greg Laurans. And already she saw signs that worried her.

She knew she would have to tell him soon. In a way that his seven-year-old mind could understand, she would have to explain to him the facts of death.

For in light of new knowledge, she was questioning everything. In those dim months when the doctors themselves, as well as Mrs. Harrington, had stopped thinking about the fact that she was to die, she had become too complacent, she had not made enough plans for what would be left after her. Die. The word struck, and bounced off her skull. Soon, she knew, when the chemotherapy began, she would start to get thinner, and her hair would fall out in greater quantities. She envisioned herself, then, months, or perhaps only weeks from now, so different—bones jutting out of skin, hair in clumps like patches of weeds on a desert. She anticipated great weariness, for she would be lucid, fiercely lucid, and though she would look like death, she would live for the day when once again she would feel well. Her friends would come to see her, frightened, needing reassurance. "You look so tired, Anna," they'd say. Then she would have to explain, It's the radiation, the drugs, it's all to make me better. And when they assailed her, begging her to complete that tantalizing hint of hopefulness so that they could leave without worry or fear for themselves, she would have to temper their desire for anything in only the middle ranges of despair; though she was getting better, she would probably be dead by next Christmas.

Dead by Christmas; she wondered if her children suspected that this would be her last Christmas. Then Jennifer would go to college, Roy and Ernest to her sister in Washington (though her ex-husband would probably fight for a custody she had made sure he would never get; she had at least covered that base).

Now she looked at her children. They ate, they gossiped between bites. Dear God, she thought, how will they get along without me? For if she had died today, they would probably be eating in a friend's kitchen—the Lauranses' or the Lewistons'—in shock, as yet not really believing she was gone. There would be the unfamiliar smell of someone else's cooking, someone else's dinner, another way of making spaghetti sauce. And at home, the unmade bed, her clothes, her *smell* still in the closet, in the bed, lingering a few days, then disappearing from the world forever. Soon Ernest would start to cry for her, and alien arms would take him up. There would be nothing she could do. She would be gone.

They didn't notice anything different. Happily eating, arguing, in the cramped kitchen full of steam and the smell of butter.

"Pass the noodles," Mrs. Harrington said.

"Mom, you never eat noodles."

She dressed in a big, dark gown with an Indian design stitched into it—a birthday present from Jennifer. A life of objects spread out before her—the bed, the television, so many cans of SpaghettiOs for Ernest. New products in the grocery store. The ads for reducer-suits in *TV Guide*.

"Mom, let's go, we're gonna be late!" Ernest shouted.

"Ern, let's watch 'The Flintstones,' " Jennifer said. To help her mother. She tried to help.

"Is Ernie dressed?" Mrs. Harrington asked.

"Yes, he is."

But when she emerged, perfumed, soft, Ernest didn't want to leave. "Dino's run away," he said.

"We have to go, Ern," Jennifer said. "Don't you want to go to the Lauranses'? Don't you want to see Timmy?"

Ernest started to cry. "I want to watch," he said in a tiny voice.

"All your friends will be at the party," Mrs. Harrington consoled.

"Oh, shit," said Roy, "why do you treat him like such a baby when he mopes like this? You're a baby," he said to his brother.

"I am not a baby," Ernest said.

"Babies cry 'cause they can't watch TV 'cause they're going to a party instead. You're a baby."

Ernest's crying got suddenly louder.

"You've done it," Jennifer said.

Thirty minutes later, Dino was safely home, and the Harringtons were on their way. Dry-eyed. "Happy now?" Mrs. Harrington asked.

Jennifer and Ernest climbed into the back. "I hope Timmy's there," Ernest said.

"Can I drive?" Roy asked.

"Not tonight, I'd be scared," Mrs. Harrington said.

"Then can we at least listen to KFRC?" Roy asked.

"Yeah! Maybe they'll have the Police!" Ernest shouted gleefully.

"O.K., sure," said Mrs. Harrington.

"You're in a good mood," said Roy, switching one of the preset buttons to the station he wanted.

They pulled out of the driveway. The dark, warm car filled up with a loud, sad song:

Why did you have to be a heartbreaker,
When I was be-ing what you want me to be . . .

Roy beat his hand against the dashboard. He looked funny in his orange shirt and green tie—long hair spilling over corduroy jacket—as if he had never been meant to dress that way and had adjusted the standard male uniform to his particular way of life.

Oh, Mrs. Harrington relished that moment: her children all around her. What amazed her was that she had made them—they wouldn't be who they were, they wouldn't be at all, if it hadn't been for her. Aside from a few sweaters and a large macramé wall hanging, they were her life's artwork. She was proud of them, and fearful.

They turned onto a dark road that twisted up into the hills. From the Lauranses' high window, Mrs. Harrington's house was one of a thousand staggered lights spreading like a sequined dress to the spill of the bay.

The Lauranses had introduced her to a woman who was involved with holistic healing. "Meditate on your cancer," the woman had said. "Imagine it. Visualize it inside of you. Then, imagine it's getting very cold. Imagine the tumors freezing, dying from freezing. Then a wind chips at them until they disappear."

"Oh," Mrs. Harrington said, overcome again. "Oh."

"Mom, what's wrong?" Roy asked her. In the dark car, concern seemed to light up his face. She could only look at him for a second because the road was curving up to meet her stare.

"Nothing," she said. "I'm sorry. Just a little pensive tonight, that's all."

But in her mind she could see Dr. Sanchez's hairy hands.

*   *   *

The party was already in full swing when they arrived. All over the Lauranses' carpeted living room the clink of drinks sounded, a slow, steady murmur of conversation. Ernest held Mrs. Harrington's hand.

She lost Jennifer and Roy instantly, lost them to the crowd, to their friends. Suddenly. They were on their own, moving in among the guests, who said hello, asked them what their plans were. They smiled. They were good kids, eager to find their friends.

"Hey, Harrington!" she heard a gravelly adolescent voice call, and Roy was gone. Jennifer lost as well, to the collegiate generation—a boy just back from Princeton.

Mrs. Harrington's friends the Lewistons were the first to greet her. Mr. Lewiston had taught in the law school with Mrs. Harrington's ex-husband, and they had remained friends.

"How are you feeling, Anna?"

"How're the kids?"

"You know, anything we can do to help."

She motioned toward Ernest with her eyes, don't talk about it. Ernest, who had not been listening, asked, "Where's Timmy?"

"Timmy and Kevin and Danielle are in the family room playing," Mrs. Lewiston said. "Would you like to join them?"

"Kevin!" Ernest turned to his mother, his eyes and mouth breaking. There was a red sore on his chin from drool. He started to cry.

"Ernie, baby, what's wrong?" Mrs. Harrington said, picking him up, hugging him fiercely.

"I don't like Kevin," Ernest sobbed. "He's mean to me."

Kevin was the Lewistons' son. As a baby, he had been on commercials.

And the Lewistons looked at Mrs. Harrington in vague horror.

"When was he mean to you?" Mrs. Harrington asked.

"The other day on the bus. He threw—um, he threw—he took my lunch and he threw it at me and it got broken. My thermos."

Mrs. Harrington looked at the Lewistons, for a brief moment accusingly, but she quickly changed her look to one of bewilderment.

"He did come home the other day with his thermos broken. Ernest, you told me you dropped it."

"Kevin told me not to tell. He—he said he'd beat me up."

"Look, Anna, how can you—how can you think . . ." Mrs. Lewiston couldn't complete her sentence. "I'll get Kevin," she said. "Your son's accused him of something he'd never do."

She ran off toward the family room.

"Anna, are you sure Ernest's not making all this up?" Mr. Lewiston asked.

"Are you accusing him of lying?" Mrs. Harrington said.

"Look, we're adults. Let's keep cool. I'm sure there's an explanation to all of this." Mr. Lewiston took out a handkerchief and swatted at his face.

Ernest was still crying when Mrs. Lewiston came back, dragging Kevin by the arm.

Ernest wailed. Mrs. Laurans, the hostess, came over to find out what was causing such a commotion. She ushered the families into the master bedroom to have it out.

"Kevin," Mr. Lewiston said, seating his son on top of forty or fifty coats piled on the bed, "Ernest has accused you of doing something very bad—of taking his lunch and hitting him with it. Is this true? Don't lie to me."

"Bill, how can you talk to him that way?" Mrs. Lewiston cried. "You're never that way with him."

Kevin, a handsome, well-dressed child, began to cry. The adults stood among their sobbing children.

"Oh dear," Mrs. Harrington said. Then she laughed just a little.

Mrs. Lewiston took her lead, and laughed, too. The tension broke.

But Mr. Lewiston, overcome by guilt for treating his son badly, was holding Kevin, and begging his forgiveness.

Mrs. Harrington knew what that was like. She also knew that Ernest had lied before. She led him over to the corner.

"Did you make that story up, Ernest?" she asked him.

"No."

"Tell the truth."

"I didn't," Ernest said.

"Kevin says you did," Mrs. Harrington said with infinite gentleness.

"He's lying."

"You can't pretend with me, young man." Her voice grew stern. "Look, I want the truth."

Sternly, she lifted up his chin so that his eyes met hers; she was on her knees. For a moment, he looked as if he might once again break out in full-fledged sobs. But Ernest changed his mind.

"All right," he said. "He didn't throw it at me. But he took it."

"I gave it back!" Kevin yelled. "I threw it *to* you, and you dropped it and the thermos broke!"

"Ah!" all the parents said at once.

"Two parties misinterpret the same incident. Happens all the time in the courts. I teach about it in my class," Mr. Lewiston said. Everyone laughed.

"Now, Mrs. Harrington, I think both these young men owe each other an apology, don't you? Kevin for taking Ernest's lunch, and Ernest for saying he threw it at him."

"Boys," Mrs. Harrington said, "will you shake hands and make up?"

The children eyed each other suspiciously.

"Come on," Mr. Lewiston said to Kevin. "Be a good cowboy, pardner."

Kevin, like a good cowboy, reached out a swaggering arm. Sheepishly, Ernest accepted it. They shook.

"All right, all right," Mrs. Lewiston said. "Now why don't you two go play with Timmy and Danielle?"

"O.K.," Kevin said. The two ran off.

"And we'll all get a drink," Mr. Lewiston said.

The adults emerged from the bedroom and made their way through the crowd. All of them were relieved not to have to face the possibility that one of their children had done something consciously malicious. But Mrs. Harrington had to admit that, of the two, Ernest had come off the more childish, the less spirited. Kevin Lewiston was energetic, attractive. He had spirit—took lunch boxes but gave them back, would go far in life. Ernest cried all the time, made more enemies than friends, kept grudges.

Small children, dressed in their best, darted between and among adult legs. Mrs. Harrington, separated from the Lewistons by a dashing three-year-old girl, found herself in front of a half-empty bowl of chopped liver.

A trio of women whose names she didn't remember greeted her, but they didn't remember her name either, so it was all right. They were talking about their children. One turned out to be the mother of the boy from Princeton. "Charlie spent the past summer working in a senator's office," she told the other women, who were impressed.

"What's your daughter doing next summer?" the woman asked Mrs. Harrington.

"Oh, probably doing what she did last summer, working at Kentucky Fried Chicken." Or, perhaps, living in another town.

The ladies made noises of approval. Then, looking over their heads to the crowd to see if her children were within earshot, Mrs. Harrington saw someone she had no desire to talk to.

"Excuse me," she hurriedly told the women. But it was too late. "Anna!"

Joan Lensky had seen her; now she was done for. Her black hair tied tightly behind her head, dressed (as always) in black, Joan Lensky was coming to greet her.

"Anna, darling," she said, grasping Mrs. Harrington's hand between sharp fingers, "I'm so glad to see you could come out." ·

"Yes, well, I'm feeling quite well, Joan," Mrs. Harrington said.

"It's been so long. Are you really well? Let's chat. There's a room over there we can go to and talk privately."

Regretfully, Mrs. Harrington was pulled away from the crowd into an empty room. She did not enjoy talking to Joan Lensky; the details of their histories, at least on the surface, bore too much resemblance to each other. Up until his death, Joan's husband had been famous for making advances to his female graduate students—so often, and so clumsily, that his lechery had become a joke at the faculty wives' teas.

Mrs. Harrington's husband was more serious; he left her suddenly and flatly for a law student, quit his job, and moved with her to Italy. After that Mrs. Harrington stopped going to the faculty wives' teas, though most of the wives remained steadfastly loyal—none more so than Joan, who seized on the wronged Mrs. Harrington as a confidante. It made Mrs. Harrington nervous to realize how much she knew about Joan's life that Joan herself didn't know—Joan, with her black poodles, her immaculate kitchen. Nevertheless, she put up with this demanding friendship for many years, chiefly because she felt sorry for the old woman, who seemed to need so badly to feel sorry for her. When she got sick she changed her priorities. Now she only saw Joan when she had to.

Tell me, then, how are you?" Mrs. Lensky asked her gravely. They were sitting on an Ultrasuede sofa in a small sitting room, close together. Mrs. Harrington could feel Mrs. Lensky's breath blowing on her face.

"I'm all right. I feel well. The kids are doing fine."

"No, no, Anna," Mrs. Lensky said, shaking her head emphatically. "How *are* you?"

She couldn't put off the inevitable any longer.

"All right. I'm on the tail end of radiation therapy. It's about fifty percent effective."

"Oh, you poor, poor dear," Mrs. Lensky said. "Is there much pain?"

"No."

"And your hair? Is that a wig?"

"No, I have it specially cut."

Mrs. Lensky looked toward the ceiling and closed her eyes rapturously.

"You are so lucky, my dear Anna, you don't know," she said. "My sister has a friend who is going through terrible ordeals with the radiation. All her hair. She weighs seventy pounds. Terrible. Don't let them increase your dose! Or that awful chemotherapy!"

"All right," Mrs. Harrington said.

"You must avoid chemotherapy. I know a woman who died from it. They said it was the treatment that killed her, because it was worse than the disease. Another woman I know was so sick she had to stay in bed for three months. She's still so pale. Also during surgery make sure they don't leave any of their sponges inside your stomach . . ."

Mrs. Harrington counted her breaths, thought, It's all she has to live for, other people's sorrows to compare with her own.

"Have you heard from Roy? Is he still married to that child?"

"Yes," Mrs. Harrington said. "He is. She's actually very nice. They're quite happy."

Mrs. Lensky nodded. Then she moved even closer to Mrs. Harrington, to deliver some even greater confidence.

"I heard of an organization I thought you would want to know about," she said. "It arranges for . . . things . . . before you go. So that your children won't have to worry about it. I'm a member. The dues aren't heavy, and they take care of everything . . . just everything."

She handed Mrs. Harrington a small slip of paper that she had produced from her purse. "That's all you need to know," she said.

At that moment, thank heavens, the door opened.

Jennifer had come to rescue her mother. To help her out.

"Mom, I need to talk to you," she said.

"I'm sorry, Joan," Mrs. Harrington said, standing. "We'll talk."

Thank you for rescuing me," Mrs. Harrington whispered to her daughter.

"Mom, you're not going to believe it," Jennifer said. "Greg Laurans is here. And he brought those people with him."

"You mean from Young Life?"

"Them . . . and some others."

In the dining room, the mass of guests had separated into small clumps, all engaged in *not* looking at the sunken bowl of the living room, *not* listening to the music rising up from it.

Mrs. Harrington glanced down curiously. Seated around the fireplace, by the Christmas tree, were Greg and a group of cherubic young people, all clean-cut, wearing little gold glasses and down vests. One had a guitar, and they were singing:

> *"And she draws dragons*
> *And dreams become real*
> *And she draws dragons*
> *To show how she feels."*

Mrs. Harrington looked behind her. Mrs. Laurans was dropping an olive into a martini; *this*, she thought, is cruel and unusual punishment.

Then she noticed the others. There were three of them. The boys were dressed neatly in sweaters. One had dark blond hair and round eyes. Occasionally the girl next to him had to take his chin between her thumb and forefinger and wipe it with a Kleenex. The other boy was darker, squatter, and could not seem to keep his head up. Every few minutes, the girl with the Kleenex would lift up his chin and he would look around himself curiously, like a child held before an aquarium. Near them was a dwarf girl with a deformed head, too large, the shape of an ostrich egg, and half of it forehead, so that the big eyes seemed to be set unnaturally low. Yet they were alert eyes, more focused than those of the boys. From the corner where they were gathered, the three sang along:

> *"An se dwaw daguhs*
> *And de becuh ree*
> *An se dwaw daguhs*
> *Ta so ha se fee."*

"They're from the state hospital," Jennifer told her mother. "They'll probably live there all their lives. It was really amazing that they let them go to come here. It's incredibly nice, really, even though it's pretty horrifying for us."

"And for Greg's mother," Mrs. Harrington said, distantly.

She stared down at the circle of singers. Now some of them were shoving pieces of paper and crayons into the invalids' hands.

> *"And she draws unicorns*
> *And makes us all free*
> *(An se dwaw oonicaws)."*

"Come on," the pretty young people were saying. "Draw a daguh. Draw an oonicaw."

"This is the cruelest thing of all," Mrs. Harrington said to her daughter.

She turned around again, but Mrs. Laurans had disappeared. Quickly she walked toward the bedroom. She rapped on the door, opened it. Ursula Laurans lay on her bed, on top of fifty or sixty coats, crying.

Mrs. Harrington sat down next to her, rubbed her back.

"I'm sorry, Ursie. I'm sorry," she said.

"Why does he do this to me?" Mrs. Laurans asked. "He was getting so much better, he went to synagogue. For Christ's sake, he was a physics major, a goddamn physics major. Then one day he comes home and he tells me he's found Jesus. He tries to convert *us*, his parents. You don't know how it upset Ted. He tried to argue with him. He wouldn't even accept the theory of evolution. A physics major! He thinks everything in the Bible is true! And now this."

"I'm sorry, Ursie," Mrs. Harrington said.

Ted Laurans entered the room. "Oh, God," he said to his wife. "Oh, God. I'll kill him. How can he do this?"

"Shut up," Ursula said. "It's futile. You gave him all that bullshit already, about questioning. He's beyond reason."

Why were they telling her this? Mrs. Harrington tried to be comforting. "Oh, Ursie," she said.

Then, very suddenly, Ursula Laurans launched up and landed against Mrs. Harrington. She fell against her, dead weight, cold and heavy. Mrs. Harrington's arms went around her instinctively.

Ted Laurans was crying, too. Standing and crying, softly, his hands over his face, the way men usually do.

"Maybe this is his way of trying to reestablish a relationship," Mrs. Harrington offered. "It's very kind, bringing them here. No other person would have done it."

"It's all aggression," Ursula said. "We've been seeing a family therapist. It's all too clear. I wasn't enough of a mother to him, so he took the first maternal substitute he came across."

Mrs. Harrington chose not to say anything more. Soon Ted Laurans ran into the bathroom, leaving the two women alone with the coats.

Eventually, Mrs. Harrington emerged. Many of the guests were leaving; in the kitchen she bumped into the dwarf girl, who was washing a glass in the sink with remarkable expertise despite the fact that her chin barely reached the counter.

"Excuse me," she said quite clearly. "I get under people's feet a lot."

They both laughed. The dwarf girl smiled pleasantly at her, and Mrs. Harrington was glad to see that she had the capacity to smile. The dwarf girl wore a houndstooth dress specially tailored for her squat body, and fake pearls. She had large breasts, which surprised Mrs. Harrington; she wore a gold necklace and a little ring on one of her fingers. Obviously she wasn't as retarded as the two boys.

Mrs. Harrington turned around to look for her children. Then Ernest ran into the kitchen. He was crying again. He held his arms out, and she lifted him up. "Oh, Ernie, you'll get sick from so much crying," she said.

"I want to go home," Ernest said.

"What's wrong? Didn't you have fun?"

"They ditched me."

"Oh, Ernie."

Three little children, two boys and a girl, ran into the kitchen, laughing, stumbling. As if she were a red light, they screeched to a halt at Mrs. Harrington's feet. "Ernie, you don't want to play anymore?" Kevin Lewiston asked. All the children's faces stared up, vaguely disturbed.

"Go away!" Ernest screamed, turning in to his mother's shoulder.

"All right, that's enough," Mrs. Harrington said. "I think you kids better find your parents."

"Yes, ma'am," they said in unison. Then all three ran out of the room.

Mrs. Harrington was left in the kitchen, holding her child like a bag of wet laundry. He would probably want to sleep in her bed tonight, as he did all those nights he had to wear the eye patch, to deflect lazy left eye syndrome. "We'll go home, Ernie," she said to him. Then she noticed the dwarf girl. She was still standing by the sink, staring up at her.

"Roy's in the bedroom with some boys and they're smoking pot," Ernie mumbled to Mrs. Harringston's shoulder, which was now soaked through with tears and drool.

"Don't be a tattletale," Mrs. Harrington whispered.

She looked down at the dwarf girl, who looked up at her. The dwarf girl held a glass of water in her tiny fat hand; the owl eyes in the huge head seemed gentle, almost pretty; in the bright light of the kitchen, she wore an expression that could have indicated extreme stupidity, or great knowledge.

Unmoving, the dwarf girl stared at Mrs. Harrington, as if the big woman were a curiosity, or a comrade in sorrow.

The Lost Cottage

T he Dempson family had spent the last half of June in a little rented cottage called "Under the Weather," near Hyannis, every summer for twenty-six years, and this year, Lydia Dempson told her son, Mark, was to be no exception. "No matter what's happened," she insisted over two thousand miles of telephone wire, "we're a family. We've always gone, and we'll continue to go." Mark knew from her voice that the matter was closed. They would go again. He called an airline and made a plane reservation. He arranged for someone to take care of his apartment. He purged the four pages of his *Week-at-a-Glance* which covered those two weeks of all appointments and commitment.

A few days later he was there. The cottage still needed a coat of paint. His parents, Lydia and Alex, sat at the kitchen table and shucked ears of corn. Alex had on a white polo shirt and a sun visor, and talked about fishing. Lydia wore a new yellow dress, and over it a fuzzy white sweater. She picked loose hairs from the ears Alex had shucked, which were pearl-white, and would taste sweet. Tomorrow

Mark's brother and sister, Douglas and Ellen, and Douglas's girl-friend, Julie, would arrive from the West Coast. It seemed like the opening scene from a play which tells the family's history by zeroing in on a few choice summer reunions, presumably culled from a long and happy series, to give the critical information. Mark had once imagined writing such a play, and casting Colleen Dewhurst as his mother, and Jason Robards as his father. The curtain rises. The lights come up to reveal a couple shucking corn . . .

Six months before, Alex and Lydia had gathered their children around another kitchen table and announced that they were getting a divorce. "For a long time, your mother and I have been caught up in providing a stable home for you kids," Alex had said. "But since you've been out on your own, we've had to confront certain things about our relationship, certain facts. And we have just decided we'd be happier if we went on from here separately." His words were memorized, as Mark's had been when he told his parents he was gay; hearing them, Mark felt what he imagined they must have felt then: not the shock of surprise, but of the unspoken being spoken, the long-dreaded breaking of a silence. Eight words, four and a half seconds: a life changed, a marriage over, three hearts stopped cold. "I can't believe you're saying this," Ellen said, and Mark knew she was speaking literally.

"For several years now," Alex said, "I've been involved with some-one else. There's no point in hiding this. It's Marian Hollister, whom you all know. Your mother has been aware of this. I'm not going to pretend that this fact has nothing to do with why she and I are divorc-ing, but I will say that with or without Marian, I think this would have been necessary, and I think your mother would agree with me on that."

Lydia said nothing. It was two days before Christmas, and the tree had yet to be decorated. She held in her hand a small gold bulb which she played with, slipping it up her sleeve and opening her fist to reveal an empty palm.

"Years," Ellen said. "You said years."

"We need you to be adults now," said Lydia. "I know this will be hard for you to adjust to, but I've gotten used to the idea, and as hard as it may be to believe, you will, too. Now a lot of work has to be done in a very short time. A lot has to be gone through. You can help by sorting through your closets, picking out what you want to save from what can be thrown away."

"You mean you're selling the house?" Mark said. His voice just barely cracked.

"The sale's already been made," Alex said. "Both your mother and I have decided we'd be happier starting off in new places."

"But how can you just sell it?" Ellen said. "You've lived here all our lives—I mean, all your lives."

"Ellen," Alex said, "you're here two weeks a year at best. I'm sorry, honey. We have to think of ourselves."

As a point of information, Douglas said, "Don't think we haven't seen what's been going on all along. We saw."

"I never thought so," Alex said.

Then Ellen asked, "And what about the cottage?"

Three months later, Alex was living with Marian in a condominium on Nob Hill, where they worked at twin oak desks by the picture window. Lydia had moved into a tiny house in Menlo Park, twenty miles down the peninsula, and had a tan, and was taking classes in pottery design. The house in which Douglas, Mark, and Ellen grew up was emptied and sold, everything that belonged to the children packed neatly in boxes and put in storage at a warehouse some-where—the stuffed animals, the old school notebooks. But none of them were around for any of that. They had gone back to Los Angeles,

Hawaii, New York—their own lives. Mark visited his mother only once, in the spring, and she took him on a tour of her new house, showing him the old dining room table, the familiar pots and pans in the kitchen, the same television set on which he had watched "Speed Racer" after school. But there was also a new wicker sofa, and everywhere the little jars she made in her pottery class. "It's a beautiful house," Mark said. "Harmonious." "That's because only one person lives here," Lydia said, and laughed. "No one to argue about the color of the drapes." She looked out the window at the vegetable garden and said, "I'm trying to become the kind of person who can live in a house like this." Mark imagined it, then; Alex and Lydia in their work clothes, sorting through twenty-six years of accumulated possessions, utility drawers, and packed closets. They had had no choice but to work through this final housecleaning together. And how had it felt? They had been married more years than he has lived.

"Under the Weather" is not the strangest name of a Cape Cod cottage, nor the most depressing. On Nantucket, for instance, there is a house called "Beyond Hope"; another called "Weak Moment"; another called "Seldom Inn." "Under the Weather" is small for such a large group, has lumpy beds and leaky faucets, but stands on a bluff, directly over a shoal where lobstermen pull up their traps. Alex and Lydia spent their honeymoon in the cottage one weekend twenty-six years ago, and loved it so much they vowed to return with their children, should they survive the war. A couple of years later, right after Lydia had Douglas, they persuaded the old woman who owned it to rent it to them for two weeks a year on a regular basis, and since then they have come every summer without fail. They hold onto the cottage as a principle, something which persists even when marriages fail, and other houses crumble. Perhaps for this reason, they have never bothered to ask anyone how it got its name. Such a question of origin interests only Mark, for whom the cottage has always been a tainted place. He remembers, as a child, coming upon his parents before dinner piercing live, writhing sea urchins with their forks, drawing them out and eating them raw. He remembers hearing them knocking about in the room next to his while he lay in bed, trying to guess if they were making love or fighting. And he remembers his own first sexual encounters, which took place near the cottage—assignations with a fisherman's son in a docked rowboat puddled with stagnant seawater. The way he figures it now, those assignations were the closest thing he has known to being in love, and his parents must have been fighting. No noise comes out of their bedroom now. Alex sleeps in the living room. What keeps Mark awake is the humming of his own brain, as he makes up new names for the place: "Desperate Efforts," perhaps, or simply, "The Lost Cottage." And what of "Under the Weather"? Who gave the cottage that name, and why? He has asked some of the lobstermen, and none of them seem to remember.

Since their arrival, Mark's parents have been distant and civil with each other, but Mark knows that no one is happy with the situation. A few weeks after he got back from his visit with his mother, Alex called him. He was in New York on business, with Marian, and they wanted Mark to have dinner with them. Mark met them at an Indian restaurant on the top of a building on Central Park South where there were gold urinals in the men's room. Marian looked fine, welcoming, and Mark remembered that before she was his father's lover, she had been his friend. That was the summer he worked as her research assistant. He also remembered that Alex almost never took Lydia with him on business trips.

"Well," Alex said, halfway through the meal, "I'll be on Cape Cod this June, as usual. Will you?"

"Dad," Mark said. "Of course."

"Of course. But Marian won't be coming, I'm afraid."

"Oh?"

"I wish she could, but your mother won't allow it."

"Really," Mark said, looking sideways at Marian for some hint as to how he should go on. She looked resolute, so he decided to be honest. "Are you really surprised?" he said.

"Nothing surprises me where your mother is concerned," Alex said. Mark supposed Alex had tried to test how far he could trespass the carefully guarded borders of Lydia's tolerance, how much he could get away with, and found he could not get away with that much. Apparently Lydia had panicked, overcome by thoughts of bedroom arrangements, and insisted the children wouldn't be able to bear Marian's presence. "And is that true?" he asked Mark, leaning toward him. "Would the children not be able to bear it?"

Mark felt as if he were being prosecuted. "I don't think Mom could bear it," he said at last—fudging, for the moment, the question of his siblings' feelings, and his own. Still, that remark was brutal enough. "Don't push it, Alex," Marian said, lighting a cigarette. "Anyway, I'm supposed to visit Kerry in Arizona that week. Kerry's living on a ranch." She smiled, retreating into the haven of her own children.

Once, Mark had been very intimate with Marian. He trusted her so much, in fact, that he came out to her before anyone else, and she responded kindly, coaxing him and giving him the strength to tell his parents he was gay. He admires her, and understands easily why his father has fallen in love with her. But since the divorce, he will not talk to Marian, for his mother's sake. Marian is the one obstacle Lydia cannot get around. Lydia never uses Marian's name because it sticks in her throat like a shard of glass and makes her cry out in pain. "Certain loyalties need to be respected" was all she could say to Alex when he suggested bringing Marian to the Cape. And Alex relented, because he agreed with her, and because he realized that two weeks in June was a small enough sacrifice, considering how far she'd stretched, how much she'd given. "Marian and I can survive," he told Mark at the Indian restaurant. "We've survived longer separations." That intimacy scalded him. As if for emphasis, Alex took Marian's hand on top of the table and held it there. "We'll survive this one," he said.

Marian laughed nervously. "Your father and I have been waiting ten years to be together," she said. "What's two weeks?"

Little about the cottage has changed since the Dempson children were children. Though Alex and Lydia talked every year about renovating, the same rotting porch still hangs off the front, the same door creaks on its hinges. The children sleep in the bedrooms they've always slept in, do the chores they've always done. "You may be adults out there," Lydia jokes, "but here you're my kids, and you do what I tell you." Ellen is a lawyer, unmarried. Two days before her scheduled departure she was asked to postpone her vacation in order to help out with an important case which was about to go to trial. She refused, and this (she thinks) might affect her chances to become a partner someday. "Ellen, why?" Mark asked her when she told him. "The family is more important," she said. "Mother is more important." Douglas has brought with him Julie, the woman he's lived with for the past five years. They do oceanographical research in a remote village on Kauai, and hold impressive fellowships. Only Mark has no career and no aspirations. He works at temporary jobs in New York and moves every few months from sublet to sublet, devoting most of his time to exploring the city's homosexual night life. For the last few months he's been working as a word processor at a bank. It was easy for him to get away. He simply quit.

Now, a week into the vacation, things aren't going well. Lydia is angry most of the time, and whenever anyone asks her why, she mentions some triviality: an unwashed pot, an unmade bed. Here is an exemplary afternoon: Douglas, Julie, Mark, and Ellen arrive back from the beach, where they've been swimming and riding waves. Lydia doesn't say hello to them. She sits, knitting, at the kitchen table. She is dressed in a fisherman's sweater and a kilt fastened with a safety pin—an outfit she saves and wears only these few weeks on the Cape. "Are we late?" Douglas asks, bewildered by her silence, out of breath.

"No," Lydia says.

"We had fun at the beach," Julie says, and smiles, unsure of herself, still a stranger in this family. "How was your day?"

"Fine," Lydia says.

Ellen rubs her eyes. "Well, Mom," she says, "would you like me to tell you I nearly drowned today? I wish I had. One less person to make a mess. Too bad Mark saved me."

Lydia puts down her knitting and cradles her face in her hands. "I don't deserve that," she says. "You don't know what it's like trying to keep ahead of the mess in this house. You have no right to make fun of me when all I'm trying to do is keep us from drowning in dirty dishes and dirty clothes."

"Didn't we do the dishes after lunch?" Douglas asks. "We must have done the dishes after lunch."

"If you can call that doing them," Lydia says. "They were soapy *and* greasy."

"I'm sorry, Lydia," says Julie. "We were in such a hurry—"

"It's just that if anything's going to get done right around here, I have to do it, and I'm sick of it. I'm sick of it." She reaches for a pack of sugarless chewing gum, unwraps a stick, and goes to work on it.

"This is ridiculous, Mom," Ellen says. "Dishes are nothing. Dishes are trivial."

"It's that attitude that gets me so riled up," Lydia says. "They're trivial to people like you, so people like me get stuck with them."

"I'm not people. I'm your daughter, Ellen, in case you've forgotten. Excuse me, I have to change."

She storms out of the kitchen, colliding with Alex, whose face and clothes are smeared with mud and sand.

"What are you in such a hurry for?" he asks.

"Ask *her*," Ellen says, and slams the door of her bedroom.

Lydia is rubbing her eyes. "What was that about?" Alex asks.

"Nothing, nothing," she says, in a weary singsong. "Just the usual. Did you fix that pipe yet?"

"No, almost. I need some help. I hoped Doug and Mark might crawl under there with me." All day he's been trying to fix a faulty pipe which has made the bathtub faucet leak for twenty-five years, and created a bluish tail of rust near the spigot. The angrier Lydia gets, the more Alex throws himself into repair work, into tending to the old anachronisms of the house which he has seen fit to ignore in other years. It gives him an excuse to spend most of his days alone, away from Lydia.

"So can you help me?" Alex asks.

"Well," Mark says, "I suppose so. When?"

"I was thinking right now. We have to get out and pick up the lobsters in an hour or so. Henry said we could ride out on the boat with him. I want to get this job done."

"Fine," Douglas, says. "I'm game."

Mark hesitates. "Yes," he says. "I'll help you with it. Just let me change first."

He walks out of the kitchen and into his bedroom. It is the smallest in the house, with a tiny child-sized bed, because even though Mark is the tallest member of the family by three inches, he is still the youngest. The bed was fine when he was five, but now most of the springs have broken, and Mark's legs stick a full four inches over the edge. He takes off his bathing suit, dries himself with a towel, and—as he dresses—catches a glimpse of himself in the mirror. It is the same face, as always.

He heads out the door to the hallway, where Alex and Douglas are waiting for him. "All right," he says. "I'm ready."

Of course, it was not this way at first. The day they arrived at the cottage, Lydia seemed exuberant. "Just breathe the air," she said to Mark, her eyes fiery with excitement. "Air doesn't smell like this anywhere else in the world." They had spaghetti with clams for dinner—a huge, decadent, drunken meal. Halfway through Mark fell to the floor in a fit of laughter so severe it almost made him sick. They went to bed at three, slept dreamlessly late into the morning. By the time Mark woke up, Lydia was irritated, and Alex had disappeared, alone, to go fishing. That evening, Ellen and Julie baked a cake, and Lydia got furious at them for not cleaning up immediately afterward. Douglas and Julie rose to the occasion, eager to appease her, and immediately started scrubbing. Douglas was even more intent than his parents on keeping up a pretense of normality over the vacation, partially for Julie's sake, but also because he cherished these two weeks at the cottage even more than his mother did. Ellen chided him for giving in to her whim so readily. "She'll just get angrier if you take away her only outlet," she said. "Leave the dirty dishes. If this house were clean, believe me, we'd get it a lot worse from her than we are now."

"I want to keep things pleasant," Douglas said. He kowtowed to his mother, he claimed, because he pitied her, but Mark knew it was because he feared more than anything seeing her lose control. When he and Douglas were children, he remembers, Lydia had been hit on the head by a softball one afternoon in the park. She had fallen to her knees and burst into tears, and Douglas had shrunk back, terrified, and refused to go near her. Now Douglas seemed determined to make sure his mother never did that to him again, even if it meant she had to suffer in silence.

Lydia is still in the kitchen, leaning against the counter, when Mark emerges from under the cottage. She is not drinking coffee, not reading a recipe; just leaning there. "Dad and Doug told me to pack up and come inside," Mark says. "I was more trouble than help."

"Oh?" Lydia says.

"Yes," Mark says, and sits down at the table. "I have no mechanical aptitude. I can hold things and hand things to other people—sometimes. They knew my heart wasn't in it."

"You never did like that sort of thing," Lydia says.

Mark sits silent for a few seconds. "Daddy's just repairing everything this vacation, isn't he?" he says. "For next summer this place'll be tiptop."

"We won't be here next summer," Lydia says. "I'm sure of it, though it's hard to imagine this is the last time."

"I'm sorry it's such an unhappy time for you," Mark says.

Lydia smiles. "Well," she says, "it's no one's fault but my own. You know, when your father first told me he wanted a divorce, he said things could be hard, or they could be very hard. The choice was up to me. I thought I chose the former of those two. Then again, I also thought, if I go along with him and don't make trouble, at least he'll be fair."

"Mom," Mark says, "give yourself a break. What did you expect?"

"I expected people to act like adults," she says. "I expected people to play fair." She turns to look out the window, her face grim. The table is strewn with gum wrappers.

"Can I help you?" Mark asks.

She laughs. "Your father would be happy to hear you say that," she says. "He told me from the beginning, I'll let them hate me, I'll turn the kids against me. Then they'll be there for you. He was so damn sacrificial. But no. You can't help me because I still have some pride."

There is a clattering of doors in the hallway. Male voices invade the house. Alex and Douglas walk into the kitchen, their clothes even more smeared with mud, their eyes triumphant. "Looks like we fixed that pipe," Alex says. "Now we've got to wash up; Henry's expecting us to pick up those lobsters ten minutes ago."

He and Douglas stand at the kitchen sink and wash their hands and faces. From her room, Julie calls, "You fixed the pipe? That's fantastic!"

"Yes," Douglas says, "we have repaired the evil leak which has plagued this house for centuries."

"We'd better get going, Doug," Alex says. "Does Julie want to come hunt lobsters?"

"Lobsters?" Julie says, entering the room. Her smile is bright, eager. Then she looks at Lydia. "No, you men go," she says. "We womenfolk will stay here and guard the hearth."

Lydia looks at her, and raises her eyebrows.

"O.K., let's go," Alex says. "Mark, you ready?"

He looks questioningly at Lydia. But she is gathering together steel wool and Clorox, preparing to attack the stain on the bathtub.

"Yes, I'm ready," Mark says.

At first, when he was very young, Mark imagined the lobstermen to be literal lobster-men, with big pink pincers and claws. Later, as he was entering puberty, he found that all his early sexual feelings focused on them—the red-faced men and boys with their bellies encased in dirty T-shirts. Here, in a docked boat, Mark made love for the first time with a local boy who had propositioned him in the bathroom of what was then the town's only pizza parlor. "I seen you look at me," said the boy, whose name was Erroll. Mark had wanted to run away, but instead made a date to meet Erroll later that night. Outside, in the pizza parlor, his family was arguing about whether to get anchovies. Mark still feels a wave of nausea run through him when he eats with them at any pizza parlor, remembering Erroll's warm breath on his neck, and the smell of fish which seemed to cling to him for days afterward.

Alex is friends with the local lobstermen, one of whom is his landlord's cousin. Most years, he and Douglas and Mark ride out on a little boat with Henry Traylor and his son, Henry Traylor, and play at being lobstermen themselves, at hauling pots and grabbing the writhing creatures and snapping shut their jaws. The lobsters only turn pink when boiled; live, they're sometimes a bluish color which reminds Mark of the stain on the bathtub. Mark has never much liked these expeditions, nor the inflated caricature of machismo which his father and brother put on for them. He looks at them and sees plump men with pale skin, men no man would ever want. Yet they are loved, fiercely loved by women.

Today Henry Traylor is a year older than the last time they saw him, as is his son. "Graduated from high school last week," he tells Alex.

"That's terrific," Alex says. "What's next?"

"Fixing to get married, I suppose," Henry Traylor says. "Go to work, have kids." He is a round-faced, red-cheeked boy with ratty, bright blond hair. As he talks, he manipulates without effort the outboard rudder of the little boat which is carrying them out into the sound, toward the marked buoys of the planted pots. Out on the ocean, Alex seems to relax considerably. "Your mother seems unhappy," he says to Mark. "I try to talk to her, to help her, but it doesn't do any good. Well, maybe Julie and Ellen can do something." He puts his arm around Mark's shoulder—an uncomplicated, fatherly gesture which seems to say, this love is simple. The love of men is simple. Leave the women behind in the kitchen, in the steam of the cooking pot, the fog of their jealousies and compulsions. We will go hunt.

Henry Traylor has hauled up the ancient lobster trap. Lobster limbs stick out of the barnacle-encrusted woodwork, occasionally moving. "Now you just grab the little bugger like this," Henry Traylor instructs Douglas. "Then you take your rubber band and snap him closed. It's simple."

"O.K.," Douglas says. "Here goes." He stands back and cranes his arm over the trap, holding himself at a distance, then withdraws a single, flailing lobster.

"Oh, God," he says, and nearly drops it.

"Don't do that!" shouts Henry Traylor. "You got him. Now just take the rubber band and fix him tight. Shut him up like he's a woman who's sassing you. That's right. Good. See? It wasn't so hard."

"Do that to your wife," says Henry Traylor the elder, "she'll bite your head off quicker than that lobster."

Out of politeness, all three of the Dempson men laugh. Douglas looks at his handiwork—a single lobster, bound and gagged—and smiles. "I did it," he says. Mark wonders if young Henry Traylor has ever thought of making love to other boys, thinks rudely of propositioning him, having him beneath the boat. "I seen you look at me," he'd say. He thinks of it—little swirls of semen coagulating in the puddles, white as the eddies of foam which are gathering now on the sea in which they float, helpless, five men wrestling with lobsters.

They go back to shore. The Traylors have asked Alex and Douglas to walk up the hill with them and take a look at their new well, so Mark carries the bag of lobsters back to the house. But when he gets to the screen door to the kitchen, he stops in his tracks; Ellen, Lydia, and Julie are sitting at the table, talking in hushed voices, and he steps back, fearful of interrupting them. "It would be all right," Ellen is saying. "Really, it's not that outrageous these days. I met a lot of really decent guys when I did it."

"What could I say?" Lydia asks.

"Just be simple and straightforward. Attractive woman, divorced, mid-fifties, seeks whatever—handsome, mature man for companionship. Who knows? Whatever you want."

"I could never put that down!" Lydia says, her inflection rising. "Besides, it wouldn't be fair. They'd be disappointed when they met me."

"Of course they wouldn't!" Julie says. "You're very attractive."

"I'm an old woman," Lydia says. "There's no need to flatter me. I know that."

"Mom, you don't look half your age," Ellen says. "You're beautiful."

Mark knocks and walks through the door, his arms full of lobsters. "Here I am," he says, "back with the loot. I'm sorry for eavesdropping, but I agree with everything Ellen says."

"Oh, it doesn't matter, Mark," Lydia says. "Alex wouldn't care anyway if he found out."

"Mom, will you stop that?" Ellen says. "Will you just stop that? Don't worry about him anymore, for Christ's sake, he isn't worth it."

"Don't talk about your father that way," Lydia says. "You can tell me whatever you think I need to know, but you're not to speak of your father like that. He's still your father, even if he's not my husband."

"Jesus," Ellen says.

"What did you say?"

"Nothing," Ellen says, more loudly.

Lydia looks her over once, then walks over to the stove, where the water for the lobsters is boiling. "How many did you get, Mark?" she asks.

"Six. Daddy and Douglas went to look at the Traylors' well. They'll be back any minute."

"Good," Lydia says. "Let's put these things in the water." She lifts the top off the huge pot, and steam pours out of it, fogging her reading glasses.

Dinner passes quietly. Alex is in a questioning mood, and his children answer him obediently. Douglas and Julie talk about the strange sleeping habits of sharks, Ellen about her firm, Mark about a play he saw recently Off Broadway. Lydia sits at the head of the table, and occasionally makes a comment or asks a question—just enough to keep them from panicking, or staring at her all through the meal. Mark notices that her eyes keep wandering to Alex.

After dinner is finished, Julie and Lydia carry the dishes into the kitchen, and Douglas says, "O.K., are we getting ice cream tonight, or what?" Every night since their arrival, they have gone to get ice cream after dinner, primarily at the insistence of Douglas and Julie, who thrive on ice cream, but thrive more on ritual. Ellen, who has visited them in Hawaii, revealed to Mark that they feed their cat tea every morning, in bed. "They're daffy," she said, describing to him the way Douglas held the cat and Julie the saucer of tea it licked from. Over the five years they've been together, Mark has noticed, Douglas and Julie have become almost completely absorbed in one another, at the expense of most everything around them, probably as a result of the fact that they've spent so much of that time in remote places, in virtual isolation. They even share a secret language of code words and euphemisms. When Julie asked Douglas, one night, to give her a "floogie," Mark burst out laughing, and then they explained that "floogie" was their private word for backrub.

Tonight, Ellen is peculiarly agreeable. Usually she resists these ice cream expeditions, but now she says, "Oh, what a great idea. Let's go." Mark wonders what led her and Lydia to the conversation he overheard, then decides he'd prefer not to know. "Let's go, let's go," Douglas says. "Mom, are you game?"

But Lydia has her face buried in the steam rising from the sink of dishes, which she has insisted on doing herself. "No," she says. "You go ahead."

Douglas backs away from the sorrow in her voice—sorrow which might at any moment turn into irritation, if he pushes her harder. He knows not to. "How about you, Dad?" he asks Alex.

"No," Alex says, "I'm pooped. But bring me back some chocolate chip."

"Give me money?" Douglas says.

Alex hands him a twenty, and the kids barrel into the car and head off to the ice cream parlor in town. They sit down at a pink booth with high-backed, patent-leather seats which remind Mark of pink flamingos on people's lawns, and a waitress in a pink uniform brings them their menus. The waitress is a local girl with bad teeth, and Mark wonders if she's the one Henry Traylor's going to marry someday. He wouldn't be surprised. She's got a lusty look about her which even he can recognize, and which he imagines Henry Traylor would find attractive. And Douglas is watching her. Julie is watching Douglas watch, but she does not look jealous. She looks fascinated.

Ellen looks jealous.

They order several sundaes, and eat them with a kind of labored dedication. Halfway through the blueberry sundae he is sharing with Ellen, Mark realizes he stopped enjoying this sundae, and this ritual, four days before. Julie looks tired, too—tired of being cheerful and shrieking about fixed faucets. And Mark imagines a time when his brother and Julie will feed their cat tea for no other reason than that they always have, and with no pleasure. He remembers one weekend when Julie and Douglas came to visit him in New York. They had taken the train down from Boston, where they were in school, and they were flying to California the next afternoon. All that day on the train Douglas had been looking forward to eating at a Southern Indian restaurant he had read about, but the train arrived several hours late, and by the time he and Julie had gotten their baggage the restaurant was closed. Douglas fumed like a child until tears came to his eyes. "All that day on the train, looking forward to that dinner," he said on the subway ride back to Mark's apartment. Julie put her arms around him, and kissed him on the forehead, but he turned away. Mark wanted to shake her, then, ask her why she was indulging him this way, but he knew that Douglas had indulged her just as often. That was the basis of their love—mutual self-indulgence so excessive that Mark couldn't live with them for more than a few days without thinking he would go crazy. It wasn't that he wasn't welcome. His presence or absence seemed irrelevent to them; as far as they were concerned, he might as well not have existed. And this was coupledom, the revered state of marriage? For Mark, the amorous maneuverings of the heterosexual world are deserving of the same bewilderment and distrust that he hears in his sister's voice when she says, "But how can you just go to bed with someone you've hardly met? *I* could never do that." He wants to respond by saying, I would never pretend that I could pledge eternal allegiance to one person, but this isn't really true. What is true is that he's terrified of what he might turn into once he'd made such a pledge.

"So when's the summit conference taking place?" Ellen says now, dropping her blueberry-stained spoon onto the pink table. Everyone looks at her. "What do you mean?" Julie asks.

"I mean I think we should have a talk about what's happening with Mom and Dad. I mean I think we should stop pretending everything's normal when it isn't."

"I'm not pretending," Douglas says.

"Neither am I," says Julie. "We're aware of what's going on."

Mark watches Ellen's blueberry ice cream melt down the sides of her parfait glass. "What has Mama said to you?" he asks.

"Everything and nothing," Ellen says. "I hear her when she's angry and when she wants to cry she does it in my room. One day she's cheerful, the next miserable. I don't know why she decided to make me her confidante, but she did." Ellen pushes the sundae dish away. "Why don't we just face the fact that this is a failure?" she says. "Daddy doesn't want to be here, that's for sure, and I think Mom's beginning to think that she doesn't want to be here. And I, for one, am not so sure I want to be here."

"Mom believes in tradition," Douglas says softly, repeating a phrase they've heard from her a thousand times.

"Tradition can become repetition," Ellen says, "when you end up holding onto something just because you're afraid to let it go." She shakes her head. "I am ready to let it go."

"Let what go?" Douglas says. "The family?"

Ellen is silent.

"Well, I don't think that's fair," Douglas says. "Sure, things are stressful. A lot has happened. But that doesn't mean we should give up. We have to work hard at this. Just because things are different doesn't mean they necessarily have to be bad. I, for one, am determined to make the best of this vacation—for my sake, but also for Mom's. Except for this, without this—"

"She already has nothing," Ellen says.

Douglas stares at her.

"You can face it," Ellen says. "She has. She's said as much. Her whole life went down the tubes when Daddy left her, Cape Cod or no Cape Cod. This vacation doesn't matter a damn. But that's not the end. She could start a new life for herself. Mark, remember the first time Douglas didn't come home for Christmas? I'll bet you never guessed how upset everyone was, Douglas. Christmas just wasn't going to be Christmas without the whole family being there, I said, so why bother having it at all? But then Christmas came, and we did it without you. It wasn't the same. But it was still Christmas. We survived. And maybe we were a little relieved to find we weren't as dependent on your presence as we thought we'd be, relieved to be able to give up some of those old rituals, some of that nostalgia. It was like a rehearsal for other losses we probably all knew we'd have to face someday—for this, maybe."

Douglas has his arm around Julie, his fingers gripping her shoulder. "No one ever told me that," he says. "I figured no one cared."

Ellen laughs. "That's never been a problem in this family," she says. "The problem in this family is that everybody cares."

They get back to the cottage around eleven to find that the lights are still on. "I'm surprised she's still up," Ellen says to Mark as they clamber out of the car.

"It's not so surprising," Mark says. "She's probably having a snack." The gravel of the driveway crunches beneath his feet as he moves toward the screen door to the kitchen. "Hi, Mom," Mark says as he walks through the door, then stops abruptly, the other three behind him.

"What's going on?" Mark asks.

Alex is standing by the ironing board, in his coat, his face red and puffy. He is looking down at Lydia, who sits in her pink bathrobe at the kitchen table, her head resting on her forearms, weeping. In front of her is half a grapefruit on a plate, and a small spoon with serrated edges.

"What happened?" Ellen asks.

"It's nothing, kids," Alex says. "Your mother and I were just having a discussion."

"Oh, shut up," Lydia says, raising her head slightly. Her eyes are red, swollen with tears. "Why don't you just tell them if you're so big on honesty all of a sudden? Your father's girlfriend has arrived. She's at a motel in town. They planned this all along, and your father never saw fit to tell any of us about it, except I happened to see her this morning when I was doing the grocery shopping."

"Oh, God," Mark says, and leans back against the wall of the kitchen. Across from him, his father also draws back.

"All right, let's not get hysterical," Ellen says. "Let's try to talk this through. Daddy, is this true?"

"Yes," Alex says. "I'm sorry I didn't tell any of you but I was afraid of how you'd react. Marian's just here for the weekend, she'll be gone Monday. I thought I could see her during the day, and no one would know. But now that everything's out, I can see that more deception was just a bad idea to begin with. And anyway, am I asking so much? All I'm asking is to spend some time in town with Marian. I'll be home for meals, and during the day, everything for the family. None of you ever has to see her."

"Do you think all this is fair to Marian?" Ellen asks.

"It was her idea."

"I see."

"Fair to Marian, fair to Marian," Lydia mumbles. "All of this has been fair to Marian. These two weeks you were supposed to be fair to me." She takes a Kleenex and rubs at her nose and eyes. Mark's fingers grip the moldings on the walls, while Julie buttons and unbuttons the collar of her sweater.

"Lydia, look," Alex says. "Something isn't clear here. When I agreed to come these weeks, it was as your friend and as a father. Nothing more."

"So go then!" Lydia shouts, standing up and facing him. "You've brought me lower than I ever thought you would, don't stand there and rub it in. Just go." Shaking, she walks over to the counter, picks up a coffee cup, and takes a sip out of it. Coffee splashes over the rim, falls in hot drops on the floor.

"Now I think we have to talk about this," Ellen says. "We can deal with this if we just work on it."

"There's no point," Douglas says, and sits down at the table. "There's nothing left to say." He looks at the table, and Julie reaches for his hand.

"What do you mean there's nothing left to say? There's everything to be said here. The one thing we haven't done is talk about all of this as a family."

"Oh, be quiet, both of you," Lydia says, putting down her cup. "You don't know anything about this. The whole business is so simple it's embarrassing." She puts her hand on her chest and takes a deep, shaky breath. "There is only one thing to be said here, and I'm the one who has to say it. And that is the simple fact that I love your father, and I will always love your father. And he doesn't love me. And never will."

No one answers her. She is right. None of them know anything about *this*, not even Ellen. Lydia's children are as speechless as spectators watching a woman on a high ledge: unable to do any good, they can only stare, waiting to see what she'll do next.

What she does is turn to Alex. "Did you hear me?" she says. "I love you. You can escape me, but you can never escape that."

He keeps his eyes focused on the window above her head, making sure never to look at her. The expression on his face is almost simple, almost sweet: the lips pressed together, though not tightly, the eyes averted. In his mind, he's already left.

Aliens

A year ago today I wouldn't have dreamed I'd be where I am now: in the recreation room on the third floor of the State Hospital, watching, with my daughter, ten men who sit in a circle in the center of the room. They look almost normal from a distance—khaki pants, lumberjack shirts, white socks—but I've learned to detect the tics, the nervous disorders. The men are members of a poetry writing workshop. It is my husband Alden's turn to read. He takes a few seconds to find his cane, to hoist himself out of his chair. As he stands, his posture is hunched and awkward. The surface of his crushed left eye has clouded to marble. There is a pale pink scar under his pale yellow hair.

The woman who leads the workshop, on a volunteer basis, rubs her forehead as she listens, and fingers one of her elephant-shaped earrings. Alden's voice is a hoarse roar, only recently reconstructed. "Goddamned God," he reads. "I'm mad as hell I can't walk or talk."

*   *   *

It is spring, and my youngest child, my eleven-year-old, Nina, has convinced herself that she is an alien.

Mrs. Tompkins, her teacher, called me in yesterday morning to tell me. "Nina's constructed a whole history," she whispered, removing her glasses and leaning toward me across her desk, as if someone might be listening from above. "She never pays attention in class, just sits and draws. Strange landscapes, star-charts, the interiors of spaceships. I finally asked some of the other children what was going on. They told me that Nina says she's waiting to be taken away by her real parents. She says she's a surveyor, implanted here, but that soon a ship's going to come and retrieve her."

I looked around the classroom; the walls were papered with crayon drawings of cars and rabbits, the world seen by children. Nina's are remote, fine landscapes done with Magic Markers. No purple suns with faces. No abrupt, sinister self-portraits. In the course of a year Nina suffered a violent and quick puberty, sprouted breasts larger than mine, grew tufts of hair under her arms. The little girls who were her friends shunned her. Most afternoons now she stands in the corner of the playground, her hair held back by barrettes, her forehead gleaming. Recently, Mrs. Tompkins tells me, a few girls with glasses and large vocabularies have taken to clustering around Nina at recess. They sit in the broken bark beneath the slide and listen to Nina as one might listen to a prophet. Her small eyes, exaggerated by her own glasses, must seem to them expressive of martyred beauty.

"Perhaps you should send her to a psychiatrist," Mrs. Tompkins suggested. She is a good teacher, better than most of her colleagues. "This could turn into a serious problem," she said.

"I'll consider it," I answered, but I was lying. I don't have the money. And besides, I know psychiatry; it takes things away. I don't think I could bear to see what would be left of Nina once she'd been purged of this fantasy.

Today Nina sits in the corner of the recreation room. She is quiet, but I know her eyes are taking account of everything. The woman with the elephant-shaped earrings is talking to one of the patients about poetry *qua* poetry.

"You know," I say to her afterward, "it's amazing that a man like Alden can write poems. He was a computer programmer. All our married life he never read a book."

"His work has real power," the teacher says. "It reminds me of Michelangelo's Bound Slaves. Its artistry is heightened by its rawness."

She hands me a sheet of mimeographed paper—some examples of the group's work. "We all need a vehicle for self-expression," she says.

Later, sitting on the sun porch with Alden, I read through the poems. They are full of expletives and filthy remarks—the kind of remarks my brother used to make when he was hot for some girl at school. I am embarrassed. Nina, curled in an unused wheelchair, is reading "The Chronicles of Narnia" for the seventeenth time. We should go home soon, but I'm wary of the new car. I don't trust its brakes. When I bought it, I tested the seatbelts over and over again.

"Dinner?" Alden asks. Each simple word, I remember, is a labor for him. We must be patient.

"Soon," I say.

"Dinner. It's all—" He struggles to find the word; his brow is red, and the one seeing eye stares at the opposite wall.

"Crap," he says. He keeps looking at the wall. His eyes are expressionless. Once again, he breathes.

Nearby, someone's screaming, but we're used to that.

A year ago today. The day was normal. I took my son, Charles, to the dentist's. I bought a leg of lamb to freeze. There was a sale on paper towels. Early in the evening, on our way to a restaurant, Alden drove the car through a fence, and over an embankment. I remember, will always remember, the way his body fell almost gracefully through the windshield, how the glass shattered around him in a thousand glittering pieces. Earlier, during the argument, he had said that seatbelts do more harm than good, and I had buckled myself in as an act of vengeance. This is the only reason I'm around to talk about it.

I suffered a ruptured spleen in the accident, and twenty-two broken bones. Alden lost half his vision, much of his mobility, and the English language. After a week in intensive care they took him to his hospital and left me to mine. In the course of the six months, three weeks, and five days I spent there, eight women passed in and out of the bed across from me. The first was a tiny, elderly lady who spoke in hushed tones and kept the curtain drawn between us. Sometimes children were snuck in to visit her; they would stick their heads around the curtain rod and gaze at me, until a hand pulled them back and a voice loudly whispered, "Sorry!" I was heavily sedated; everything seemed to be there one minute, gone the next. After the old woman left, another took her place. Somewhere in the course of those months a Texan mother arrived who was undergoing chemotherapy, who spent her days putting on make-up, over and over again, until, by dusk, her face was the color of bruises.

My hospital. What can you say about a place to which you become addicted? That you hate it, yet at the same time, that you need it. For weeks after my release I begged to be readmitted. I would wake crying, helplessly, in the night, convinced that the world had stopped, and I had been left behind, the only survivor. I'd call the ward I had lived on. "You'll be all right, dear," the nurses told me. "You don't have to come back, and besides, we've kicked you out." I wanted cups of Jell-O. I wanted there to be a light in the hall at night. I wanted to be told that six months hadn't gone by, that it had all been, as it seemed, a single, endless moment.

To compensate, I started to spend as much time as I could at Alden's hospital. The head nurse suggested that if I was going to be there all day, I might as well do something productive. They badly needed volunteers on the sixth floor, the floor of the severely retarded, the unrecoverable ones. I agreed to go in the afternoons, imagining story corner with cute three-year-olds and seventy-year-olds. The woman I worked with most closely had been pregnant three times in the course of a year. Her partner was a pale-skinned young man who drooled constantly and could not keep his head up. Of course she had abortions. None of the administrators were willing to solicit funds for birth control because that would have meant admitting there was a need for birth control. We couldn't keep the couple from copulating. They hid in the bushes and in the broom closet. They were obsessive about their lovemaking, and went to great lengths to find each other. When we locked them in separate rooms, they pawed the doors and screamed.

The final pregnancy was the worst because the woman insisted that she wanted to keep the baby, and legally she had every right. Nora, my supervisor—a crusty, ancient nurse—had no sympathy, insisted that the woman didn't even know what being pregnant meant. In the third month, sure enough, the woman started to scream and wouldn't be calmed. Something was moving inside her, something she was afraid would try to kill her. The lover was no help. Just as easily as he'd begun with her, he'd forgotten her, and taken up with a Down syndrome dwarf who got transferred from Sonoma.

The woman agreed to the third abortion. Because it was so late in the pregnancy, the procedure was painful and complicated. Nora shook her head and said, "What's the world coming to?" Then she returned to her work.

I admire women who shake their heads and say, "What's the world coming to?" Because of them, I hope, it will always stop just short of getting there.

Lately, in my own little ways, I, too, have been keeping the earth in orbit. Today, for instance, I take Alden out to the car and let him sit in the driver's seat, which he enjoys. The hot vinyl burns his thighs. I calm him. I sit in the passenger seat, strapped in, while he slowly turns the wheel. He stares through the windshield at the other cars in the parking lot, imagining, perhaps, an endless landscape unfolding before him as he drives.

Visiting hours end. I take Alden in from the parking lot, kiss him goodbye. He shares a room these days with a young man named Joe, a Vietnam veteran prone to motorcycle accidents. Because of skingrafting, Joe's face is six or seven different colors—beiges and taupes, mostly—but he can speak, and has recently regained the ability to smile. "Hey, pretty lady," he says as we walk in. "It's good to see a pretty lady around here."

Nina is sitting in the chair by the window, reading. She is sulky as we say goodbye to Alden, sulky as we walk out to the car. I suppose I should expect moodiness—some response to what she's seen this last year. We go to pick up Charles, who is sixteen and spends most of his time in the Olde Computer Shoppe—a scarlet, plum-shaped building which serves as a reminder of what the fifties thought the future would look like. Charles is a computer prodigy, a certified genius, nothing special in our circuit-fed community. He has some sort of deal going with the owner of the Computer Shoppe which he doesn't like to talk about. It involves that magical stuff called software. He uses the Shoppe's terminal and in exchange gives the owner a cut of his profits, which are bounteous. Checks arrive for him every day—from Puerto Rico, from Texas, from New York. He puts the money in a private bank account. He says that in a year he will have enough saved to put himself through college—a fact I can't help but appreciate.

The other day I asked him to please explain in English what it is that he does. He was sitting in my kitchen with Stuart Beckman, a fat boy with the kind of wispy mustache that indicates a willful refusal to begin shaving. Stuart is the dungeon master in the elaborate medieval wargames Charles's friends conduct on Tuesday nights. Charles is Galadrian, a lowly elfin-warrior with minimal experience points. "Well," Charles said, "let's just say it's a step toward the great computer age when we won't need dungeon masters. A machine will create for us a whole world into which we can be transported. We'll live inside the machine—for a day, a year, our whole lives—and we'll live the adventures the machine creates for us. We're at the forefront of a major breakthrough—artificial imagination. The possibilities, needless to say, are endless."

"You've invented that?" I asked, suddenly swelling with Mother Goddess pride.

"The project is embryonic, of course," Charles said. "But we're getting there. Give it fifty years. Who knows?"

Charles is angry as we drive home. He sifts furiously through an enormous roll of green print-out paper. As it unravels, the paper flies in Nina's hair, but she is oblivious to it. Her face is pressed against the window so hard that her nose and lips have flattened out.

I consider starting up a conversation, but as we pull into the driveway I, too, feel the need for silence. Our house is dark and unwelcoming tonight, as if it is suspicious of us. As soon as we are in the door, Charles disappears into his room, and the world of his mind. Nina sits at the kitchen table with me until she has finished her book. It is the last in the Narnia series, and as she closes it, her face takes on the disappointed look of someone who was hoping something would never end. Last month she entered the local library's Read-a-Thon. Neighbors agreed to give several dollars to UNICEF for every book she read, not realizing that she would read fifty-nine.

It is hard for me to look at her. She is sullen, and she is not pretty. My mother used to say it's one thing to look ugly, another to act it. Still, it must be difficult to be betrayed by your own body. The cells divide, the hormones explode; Nina had no control over the timing, much less the effects. The first time she menstruated she cried not out of fear but because she was worried she had contracted that disease which causes children to age prematurely. We'd seen pictures of them—wizened, hoary four-year-olds, their skin loose and wrinkled, their teeth already rotten. I assured her that she had no such disease, that she was merely being precocious, as usual. In a few years, I told her, her friends would catch up.

She stands awkwardly now, as if she wants to maintain a distance even from herself. Ugliness really is a betrayal. Suddenly she can trust nothing on earth; her body is no longer a part of her, but her enemy.

"Daddy was glad to see you today, Nina," I say.

"Good."

"Can I get you anything?"

She still does not look at me. "No," she says. "Nothing."

Later in the evening, my mother calls to tell me about her new cordless electric telephone. "I can walk all around the house with it," she says. "Now, for instance, I'm in the kitchen, but I'm on my way to the bathroom." Mother believes in Christmas newsletters, and the forces of fate. Tonight she is telling me about Mr. Garvey, a local politician and neighbor who was recently arrested. No one knows the details of the scandal; Mother heard somewhere that the boys involved were young, younger than Charles. "His wife just goes on, does her gardening as if nothing happened," she tells me. "Of course, we don't say anything. What could we say? She knows we avoid mentioning it. Her house is as clean as ever. I even saw *him* the other day. He was wearing a sable sweater just like your father's. He told me he was relaxing for the first time in his life, playing golf, gardening. She looks ill, if you ask me. When I was your age I would have wondered how a woman could survive something like that, but now it doesn't surprise me to see her make do. Still, it's shocking. He always seemed like such a family man."

"She must have known," I say. "It's probably been a secret between them for years."

"I don't call secrets any basis for a marriage," Mother says. "Not in her case. Not in yours, either."

Lately she's been convinced that there's some awful secret between Alden and me. I told her that we'd had a fight the night of the accident, but I didn't tell her why. Not because the truth was too monumentally terrible. The subject of our fight was trivial. Embarrassingly trivial. We were going out to dinner. I wanted to go to a Chinese place. Alden wanted to try an Italian health food restaurant that a friend of his at work had told him about. Our family has always fought a tremendous amount about restaurants. Several times, when the four of us were piled in the car, Alden would pull off the road. "I will not drive with this chaos," he'd say. The debates over where to eat usually ended in tears, and abrupt returns home. The children ran screaming to their rooms. We ended up eating tunafish.

Mother is convinced I'm having an affair. "Alden's still a man," she says to me. "With a man's needs."

We have been talking so long that the earpiece of the phone is sticking to my ear. "Mother," I say, "please don't worry. I'm hardly in shape for it."

She doesn't laugh. "I look at Mrs. Garvey, and I'm moved," she says. "Such strength of character. You should take it as a lesson. Before I hang up, I want to tell you about something I read, if you don't mind."

My mother loves to offer information, and has raised me in the tradition. We constantly repeat movie plots, offer authoritative statistics from television news specials. "What did you read, Mother?" I ask.

"There is a man who is studying the Holocaust," she says. "He makes a graph. One axis is fulfillment/despair, and the other is success/failure. That means that there are four groups of people—those who are fulfilled by success, whom we can understand, and those who are despairing even though they're successful, like so many people we know, and those who are despairing because they're failures. Then there's the fourth group—the people who are fulfilled by failure, who don't need hope to live. Do you know who those people are?"

"Who?" I ask.

"Those people," my mother says, "are the ones who survived."

There is a long, intentional silence.

"I thought you should know," she says, "that I am now standing outside, on the back porch. I can go as far as seven hundred feet from the house."

Recently I've been thinking often about something terrible I did when I was a child—something which neither I nor Mother has ever really gotten over. I did it when I was six years old. One day at school my older sister, Mary Elise, asked me to tell Mother that she was going to a friend's house for the afternoon to play with some new Barbie dolls. I was mad at Mother that day, and jealous of Mary Elise. When I got home, Mother was feeding the cat, and without even saying hello (she was mad at me for some reason, too) she ordered me to take out the garbage. I was filled with rage, both at her and my sister, whom I was convinced she favored. And then I came up with an awful idea. "Mother," I said, "I have something to tell you." She turned around. Her distracted face suddenly focused on me. I realized I had no choice but to finish what I'd started. "Mary Elise died today," I said. "She fell off the jungle gym and split her head open."

At first she just looked at me, her mouth open. Then her eyes—I remember this distinctly—went in two different directions. For a brief moment, the tenuousness of everything—the house, my life, the universe—became known to me, and I had a glimpse of how easily the fragile network could be exploded.

Mother started shaking me. She was making noises but she couldn't speak. The minute I said the dreaded words I started to cry; I couldn't find a voice to tell her the truth. She kept shaking me. Finally I managed to gasp, "I'm lying, I'm lying. It's not true." She stopped shaking me, and hoisted me up into the air. I closed my eyes and held my breath, imagining she might hurl me down against the floor. "You monster," she whispered. "You little bastard," she whispered between clenched teeth. Her face was twisted, her eyes glistening. She hugged me very fiercely and then she threw me onto her lap and started to spank me. "You monster, you monster," she screamed between sobs. "Never scare me like that again, never scare me like that again."

By the time Mary Elise got home, we were composed. Mother had made me swear I'd never tell her what had happened, and I never have. We had an understanding, from then on, or perhaps we had a secret. It has bound us together, so that now we are much closer to each other than either of us is to Mary Elise, who married a lawyer and moved to Hawaii.

The reason I cannot forget this episode is because I have seen, for the second time, how easily apocalypse can happen. That look in Alden's eyes, the moment before the accident, was a look I'd seen before.

*   *   *

I hear you're from another planet," I say to Nina after we finish dinner.

She doesn't blink. "I assumed you'd find out sooner or later," she says. "But, Mother, can you understand that I didn't want to hurt you?"

I was expecting confessions and tears. Nina's sincerity surprises me. "Nina," I say, trying to affect maternal authority, "tell me what's going on."

Nina smiles. "In the Fourth Millennium," she says, "when it was least expected, the Brolian force attacked the city of Landruz, on the planet Abdur. Chaos broke loose all over. The star-worms escaped from the zoo. It soon became obvious that the community would not survive the attack. Izmul, the father of generations, raced to his space-cruiser. It was the only one in the city. Hordes crowded to get on board, to escape the catastrophe and the star-worms, but only a few hundred managed. Others clung to the outside of the ship as it took off and were blown across the planet by its engines. The space-cruiser broke through the atmosphere just as the bomb hit. A hundred people were cast out into space. The survivors made it to a small planet, Dandril, and settled there. These are my origins."

She speaks like an oracle, not like anything I might have given birth to. "Nina," I say, "*I* am your origin."

She shakes her head. "I am a surveyor. It was decided that I should be born in earthly form so that I could observe your planet and gather knowledge for the rebuilding of our world. I was generated in your womb while you slept. You can't remember the conception."

"I remember the exact night," I say. "Daddy and I were in San Luis Obispo for a convention."

Nina laughs. "It happened in your sleep," she says. "An invisible ray. You never felt it."

What can I say to this? I sit back and try to pierce through her with a stare. She isn't even looking at me. Her eyes are focused on a spot of green caught in the night outside the window.

"I've been receiving telepathic communications," Nina says. "My people will be coming any time to take me, finally, to where I belong. You've been good to this earthly shell, Mother. For that, I thank you. But you must understand and give me up. My people are shaping a new civilization on Dandril. I must go and help them."

"I understand," I say.

She looks at me quizzically. "It's good, Mother," Nina says. "Good that you've come around." She reaches toward me, and kisses my cheek. I am tempted to grab her the way a mother is supposed to grab a child—by the shoulders, by the scruff of the neck; tempted to bend her to my will, to spank her, to hug her.

But I do nothing. With the look of one who has just been informed of her own salvation, the earthly shell I call Nina walks out the screen door, to sit on the porch and wait for her origins.

Mother calls me again in the morning. "I'm in the garden," she says, "looking at the sweetpeas. Now I'm heading due west, toward where those azaleas are planted."

She is preparing the Christmas newsletter, wants information from my branch of the family. "Mother," I say, "it's March. Christmas is months away." She is unmoved. Lately, this business of recording has taken on tremendous importance in her life; more and more requires to be saved.

"I wonder what the Garveys will write this year," she says. "You know, I just wonder what there is to say about something like that. Oh my. There he is now, Mr. Garvey, talking to the paper boy. Yes, when I think of it, there have been signs all along. I'm waving to him now. He's waving back. Remember, don't you, what a great interest he took in the Shepards' son, getting him scholarships and all? What if they decided to put it all down in the newsletter? It would be embarrassing to read."

As we talk, I watch Nina, sitting in the dripping spring garden, rereading *The Lion, the Witch and the Wardrobe*. Every now and then she looks up at the sky, just to check, then returns to her book. She seems at peace.

"What should I say about your family this year?" Mother asks. I wish I knew what to tell her. Certainly nothing that could be typed onto purple paper, garnished with little pencil drawings of holly and wreaths. And yet, when I read them over, those old newsletters have a terrible, swift power, each so innocent of the celebrations and catastrophes which the next year's letter will record. Where will we be a year from today? What will have happened then? Perhaps Mother won't be around to record these events; perhaps I won't be around to read about them.

"You, can talk about Charles," I say. "Talk about how he's inventing an artificial imagination."

"I must be at least seven hundred feet from the house now," Mother says. "Can you hear me?"

Her voice is crackly with static, but still audible.

"I'm going to keep walking," Mother says. "I'm going to keep walking until I'm out of range."

That night in San Luis Obispo, Alden—can you remember it? Charles was already so self-sufficient then, happily asleep in the little room off ours. We planned that night to have a child, and I remember feeling sure that it would happen. Perhaps it was the glistening blackness outside the hotel room window, or the light rain, or the heat. Perhaps it was the kind of night when spaceships land and aliens prowl, fascinated by all we take for granted.

There are some anniversaries which aren't so easy to commemorate. This one, for instance: one year since we almost died. If I could reach you, Alden, in the world behind your eyes, I'd ask you a question: Why did you turn off the road? Was it whim, the sudden temptation of destroying both of us for no reason? Or did you hope the car would bear wings and engines, take off into the atmosphere, and propel you—us—in a split second, out of the world?

I visit you after lunch. Joe doesn't bother to say hello, and though I kiss you on the forehead, you, too, choose not to speak. "Why so glum?" I ask. "Dehydrated egg bits for breakfast again?"

You reach into the drawer next to your bed, and hand me a key. I help you out, into your bathrobe, into the hall. We must be quiet. When no nurses are looking, I hurry us into a small room where sheets and hospital gowns are stored. I turn the key in the lock, switch on the light.

We make a bed of sheets on the floor. We undress; and then, Alden, I begin to make love to you—you, atop me, clumsy and quick as a teenager. I try to slow you down, to coach you in the subtleties of love, the way a mother teaches a child to walk. You have to relearn this language as well, after all.

Lying there, pinned under you, I think that I am grateful for gravity, grateful that a year has passed and the planet has not yet broken loose from its tottering orbit. If nothing else, we hold each other down.

You look me in the eyes and try to speak. Your lips circle the unknown word, your brow reddens and beads with sweat. "What, Alden?" I ask. "What do you want to say? Think a minute." Your lips move aimlessly. A drop of tearwater, purely of its own accord, emerges from the marbled eye, snakes along a crack in your skin.

I stare at the ruined eye. It is milky white, mottled with blue and gray streaks; there is no pupil. Like our daughter, Alden, the eye will have nothing to do with either of us. I want to tell you it looks like the planet Dandril, as I imagine it from time to time—that ugly little planet where even now, as she waits in the garden, Nina's people are coming back to life.

Danny in Transit

D anny's cousins, Greg and Jeff, are playing catch. A baseball arcs over the green lawn between them, falls into the concavity of each glove with a soft thump, and flies again. They seem to do nothing but lift their gloves into the ball's path; it moves of its own volition.

Danny is lying facedown on the diving board, his hands and feet dangling over the sides, watching the ball. Every few seconds he reaches out his hands, so that his fingers brush the surface of the pool. He is trying to imagine the world extending out from where he lies: the Paper Palace, and the place he used to live, and the Amboys, Perth and South. Then Elizabeth. Then West New York. Then New York, Long Island, Italy. He listens to the sucking noise of the wind the ball makes, as it is softly swallowed. He listens to his cousins' voices. And then he takes tight hold of the diving board and tries to will it into flight, imagining it will carry him away from this back yard. But the sounds persist. He isn't going anywhere.

The huge back yard is filled with chilly New Jersey light, elegant as if it were refracted off the surface of a pearl. Carol and Nick, his aunt and uncle, sip tomato juice under an umbrella. Nearby, but separate, Elaine, Danny's mother, stares at nothing, her lips slightly parted, her mouth asleep, her eyes taking account. All that is between them is a plate of cheese.

"We went to a new restaurant, Elaine," Carol says. She is rubbing Noxzema between her palms. "Thai food. Peanut sauce and—oh, forget it."

"Keep that pitch steady, buddy," Nick calls to his sons. "Good wrist action, remember, that's the key." Both of the boys are wearing T-shirts which say *Coca-Cola* in Arabic.

"What can I do?" Carol asks.

"She's not going to talk. I don't see why we have to force her." Nick turns once again to admire his children.

"Greg, Jeff, honey, why don't you let Danny play with you?" Carol calls to her sons. They know Danny too well to take her request seriously, and keep throwing. "Come on, Danny," Carol says. "Wouldn't you like to play?"

"No, no, no, no, no," Danny says. He is roaring, but his mouth is pressed so tightly against the diving board that his voice comes out a hoarse yowl. Such an outburst isn't hard for Danny to muster. He is used to bursting into tears, into screams, into hysterical fits at the slightest inclination.

Nick gives Carol a wearied look and says, "Now you've done it." Danny bolts up from the diving board and runs into the house.

Carol sighs, takes out a Kleenex, and swats at her eyes. Nick looks at Elaine, whose expression has not changed.

"He's your son," Nick says.

"What?" says Elaine, touching her face like a wakened dreamer. Carol rocks her face in her hands.

*　　*　　*

Belle, Danny's grandmother, is in the kitchen, pulling burrs from the dog and cooking lunch, when Danny runs by. "Danny! What's wrong?" she shouts, but he doesn't answer, and flies through the door at the back of the kitchen into the room where he lives. Once inside, he dives into the big pink bed, with its fancy dust ruffle and lace-trimmed pillows; he breathes in the clean smell of the linen. It is Belle's room, the maid's quarters made over for her widowhood, and it is full of photographs of four generations of champion Labrador retrievers. When Danny arrived he was supposed to live with Greg and Jeff in their room, but he screamed so loudly that Belle—exhausted—said he could sleep in her room, and she would sleep with her other grandsons—at least for the time being. It has been two months, and Danny has not relented.

Belle is pulling burrs from her pants suit. "I'm coming in, Danny," she says, and he buries his face—hard—in the pillow. He has learned that he can usually make himself cry by doing this, even when he is actually feeling happy. The trick is to clench your eyes until a few drops of water squeeze out. And then it just happens.

Danny feels hot breath on his hair, and a soft body next to his on the bed. Belle crawls and eases her way around him, making the bed squeak, until her wet mouth is right at his ear. "What's wrong, sweetie pie?" she whispers, but he doesn't answer, only moans into his pillow.

Belle gets up abruptly. "Oh, Danny," she says, "things would be so much easier if you'd just be nice. What happened to the old Danny I used to know? Don't you know how much happier everyone else would be if you'd just be happy?"

"I hate baseball," Danny says.

Danny is an only child and he looks like the perfect combination of his two parents. His eyes are round and blue, like his mother's, his mouth small and pouting, like his father's, and his wavy brown hair halfway between Elaine's, which is red and packed in tight curls, and Allen's, which is black and straight and dense. Growing up, Danny rarely saw his parents together, and so he doesn't know the extent to which he resembles them. He remembers that his father would come home from work and insist that Danny not disturb him. In those days Allen believed that when a man got back to the house in the evening he deserved time alone with his wife as a reward for his labors. Every night Elaine ate two dinners—SpaghettiOs or Tater Tots with Danny, at six, and later, after Danny had gone to bed, something elaborate and romantic, by candlelight, with Allen. She would usually talk about the later dinners with Danny during the earlier ones. "Your father's very demanding," she said once, proudly. "He has strict notions of what a wife should do. Tonight I'm making chicken cacciatore." Danny knows that both he and his mother must have been very young when she said this, because he remembers the dreamy deliberateness with which Elaine pronounced "cacciatore," as if it were a magical incantation.

Sometimes, before Elaine put Danny to bed, Allen would pick him up and twirl him around and make sounds like an airplane. Danny slept. Through the open crack in his bedroom door he could see the candles flickering.

As he grew up Danny got to know his mother better. Starting when he was six or seven she lost her enthusiasm for dinner. "I can't manage you, Danny," she'd grumble to him. "I can't manage children. I'm unfit." Danny thought of how she always wrote DANNY G. on his lunchbag (and would continue to do so, even when he entered middle school, where last names matter). He thought of the way she made his lunch each day—peanut butter sandwich, apple, bag of cheese puffs, paper napkin. The candlelit dinners stopped, and Danny, who had never attended any of them, probably missed the ritual more than either of his parents. The three of them ate together, now, usually in silence. In those days, Elaine had a habit of staring darkly at Allen when he wasn't looking. Danny remembers Allen's anxious looks back, when he caught her face full of questions, before she shifted her eyes and changed the subject. In retrospect, Danny knows that his mother was trying to guess something, and that his father was trying to figure out how much she already knew. "I still wanted to cover my tracks," Allen recently told his son. "I knew it was futile. I knew there was no going back. I don't think I even wanted to go back. But I still covered my tracks. It becomes a habit when you do it your whole life."

One day Danny's mother did not show up to pick him up at day camp. It was getting dark, and he was the only one left. The counselor who had stayed behind began to grow impatient. Watching the sky darken, Danny felt more embarrassment than fear. He was worried that Elaine would be misconstrued as the neglectful mother she believed herself to be, and he knew her not to be.

He lied. "Oh, I forgot," he said. "She had a doctor's appointment. She said I should ask you to drive me home."

"Drive you home?" the counselor said. "Why didn't she send a note?"

"I guess she just thought you would," Danny said.

The counselor looked at him, her face full of confusion, and the beginnings of pity. Perhaps she would call child welfare. Perhaps he would be taken away. But nothing happened. She drove him home. His mother offered no explanation for what she had done, but she did not forget to pick him up again. Danny was relieved. He had feared that she would break down, sobbing, and say to the counselor, "I'm an unfit mother. Take him away."

Somehow they survived the winter. One night at dinner, a few days before spring vacation, Elaine stood up and said, "This is a sham." Then she sat down again and continued eating. Allen looked at her, looked at Danny, looked at his plate. A few nights later she picked up the top of a ceramic sugar bowl which Danny had made her for Christmas and threw it overhand at Allen. It missed him, and shattered against the refrigerator door. Danny jumped, and fought back tears.

"See what I can do?" she said. "See what you've driven me to?"

Allen did not answer her. He quietly put on his jacket, and without a word walked out the back door. He was not home for dinner the next night. When Danny asked Elaine where he'd gone, she threw down her fork and started to cry. "Danny," she said, "there have been a lot of lies in this house."

The next day was the first Monday of vacation, and when Danny came home from playing his mother was still in bed.

"It's O.K., Danny," she said. "I just decided to take the day off. Lie in bed all day, since it's something I've never done before. Don't worry about me. Go ahead and play."

Danny did as she said. That night, at dusk, when he got home, she was asleep, the lights in her room all turned out. He was frightened, and he kept the house lights on even after he'd gone to bed. In the morning he knew that his father was really gone. Only his mother was in the bed when he gently pushed open the door. "I'm not getting up again," she said. "Are you all right, honey? Can you go to the Kravitzes' for dinner?"

"Don't you want anything to eat?" Danny asked.

"I'm not hungry. Don't worry about me."

Danny had dinner with the Kravitzes. Later, returning home, he heard her crying, but he couldn't hear her after he turned on "Star Trek."

Every afternoon for a week he stood in the threshold of her doorway and asked if she wanted to get up, or if she wanted something to eat. He bought SpaghettiOs and Doritos with the money in the jar at the back of the pantry he was not supposed to know about. He never asked where his father was. Her room was musty from the closed windows, and even in the morning full of that five o'clock light which is darker than darkness, and in which the majority of car accidents happen. "Leave me alone," she would call out from the dark now. "I'm tired. For Christ's sake, just let me get some sleep. Go play or something."

Then he would close the door and make himself some Campbell's soup and watch forbidden TV all night—variety shows and detective shows and reruns after eleven. Elaine had always allotted him three hours of TV per day; when she came home from shopping she'd feel the TV to see if it was warm, if he'd been cheating. Now there were no rules.

The first day of school—a week after Elaine had gone to bed—Danny woke up to hear her screaming. He ran to her bedroom, and found her sitting up on the bed, streaked in light. She had ripped the curtains open, and the bared morning sun, through the shutters, bisected her face, the mat of her unwashed hair, the nightgown falling over her shoulders. She sat there and screamed, over and over again, and Danny rushed in, shouting, "What's wrong? What's wrong?"

And then she grabbed the ends of her hair and began tearing at them, and grinding her teeth together, and wailing. Finally she collapsed, in tears, onto the bed. She turned to look at Danny and she screamed, "I can't change! Don't you see, no matter how much I want to, I just can't change!"

Danny got Mrs. Kravitz. She came over and hoisted Elaine out of bed and began marching her around the hall. "One, two, three, let's go, let's go," Mrs. Kravitz said. "Danny, go look in the bathroom for empty pill bottles, sweetheart, your mommy's going to be just fine."

Danny didn't find any empty pill bottles, and when he came out of the bathroom some paramedics were coming through the kitchen with a stretcher. "I can't stand up," Elaine was telling Mrs. Kravitz. "I'll be sick."

"Just lie down now," Mrs. Kravitz said. Danny remembered that today was the first day of school, and he wondered whether he should go to his homeroom class or not, but when he looked at the clock, he saw that it was already eight o'clock. School had started.

Danny spent the night at the Kravitzes' house, and the next day he went to Nick and Carol's. This was in a different school district, but nobody talked about school. That night, when his cousins wanted to watch a different television show from Danny, he threw his first fit.

A few days later, while he was eating his cereal at the kitchen table, Danny's father arrived. Danny didn't say hello. He continued to spoon the sweet milk into his mouth, though the cereal was gone. Belle, who was making pancakes, turned the burner off and quietly slunk out of the room. Allen sat down across from Danny, holding a cup of coffee. He had a new short haircut, and was growing a stubbly beard. They were alone in the room.

"I know you're angry," Allen said. "I know you wonder where I've been and why your mother got sick. I don't know where to begin, and I don't expect instant forgiveness, but I do want you to hear me out. Will you do that for me? I know you'll have a lot of questions, and I'm prepared to answer them. Just give me a chance."

Danny looked at his father and didn't say anything.

On weekends Danny went to visit his father in the city. Allen was living with a man named Gene in an apartment in Greenwich Village, and though he had quit being a stockbroker, he continued to live off his own investments. Each Friday Danny rode the train up, past the fast-food franchises thrown up around the railroad stations, the muddy Amboys, the rows of tenements in Elizabeth. Allen took him to museums, to the theater, to restaurants. On Sunday he saw his son off at Penn Station. "I used to ride this train every day," he told Danny, as they waited on the platform. "I used to play cards with Uncle Nick on this train. It seems like hundreds of years."

"That was when you and Mom had dinner by candlelight," Danny said, remembering how his father twirled him in the air, how his mother pronounced the word "cacciatore"—slowly, and with such relish.

"We were innocent," Allen said. "Your mother and I believed in something that was wrong for us. Wrong for me, I should say."

Danny looked away from his father, toward the train which was now moving into the station.

"You probably think your mother's getting sick is the result of my being gay," Allen said, putting his hand on his son's shoulder. "But that's only partially true. It goes much further, much deeper than that, Danny. You know your mother hasn't been well for a long time."

From where he's lying, his face against the pillow, Danny hears the harsh sound of tires against gravel, and bolts up in bed. Through his window he sees a taxi in the driveway, and Allen, dressed in blue-jeans and a lumberjack shirt, fighting off Belle's furious barking dog. Elaine, seeing Allen, has crawled up on her haunches, and is hugging her knees. When Allen sees Elaine, he turns to rehail the taxi, but it is already out of the driveway.

"Now, Allen, don't be upset," Nick says, walking out onto the gravel, taking Allen's shoulder in one hand, the dog in the other.

"You didn't tell me she was going to be here," Allen says.

"That's because you wouldn't have come out," says Carol, joining them. "You two have to talk. We're sorry to do this, but it's the only way. Someone's got to take some responsibility."

As if he is a child about to ride a bicycle for the first time without training wheels, Allen is literally pushed by Carol toward his wife.

"What's going on? What's happening here?" shouts Belle. When she sees Allen, she stops dead in her tracks.

"You didn't tell him?" Belle asks.

Allen begins to move uncertainly toward Elaine, who is still rearing, and Carol and Nick push Belle into the kitchen. Danny jumps out of his bed and kneels next to the door.

They whisper. Nick nods and walks outdoors. "Relax, Mom," says Carol. "They've got to talk. They've got to make some decisions."

"Elaine's hospitalized." Belle announces this known fact in a low voice, and looks toward the door to her room.

"She's been hiding her whole life. She's got to face up to facts. I can't take this much longer." Carol lights a cigarette, and rubs her eyes.

Belle looks away. "He's just a child," she says.

"Their child," Carol says. "Not ours."

"Not so loudly!" Belle says, and points to the bedroom door. "Have some sympathy. She's been through a personal hell."

"I know things were hard," Carol says. "But to commit herself! I'm sorry, Mom, but as far as I'm concerned, that's just self-dramatizing. No one commits themselves these days. You see a psychiatrist on Central Park West once a week. You continue your life, and you deal with your problem."

"Her problem is worse than that," Belle says. "She needs help. All my life I never said so, but I knew she was—not strong. And now I have to admit, knowing she's taken care of, I feel relieved."

"But it's not like she's crazy!" Carol says. "It's not like she's a raving lunatic, or schizophrenic, or anything. She's basically just fine, isn't she? She just needs some help, doesn't she?"

Belle doesn't answer. Carol sits down, lays her head on the kitchen table, and starts to cry.

"Oh, my poor girl," Belle says, and strokes her daughter's hair. "I know you're worried about your sister. And she is fine. She'll be fine."

"Then why can't she just check herself out of that hospital and take her kid and start seeing a goddamned shrink once a week?" Carol says, lifting up her head and turning to face her mother. "I'll pay for it, if that's what she needs."

"Keep your voice down!" Belle whispers loudly. "Let's talk outside."

She pulls Carol out of her chair, and out the screen door. As soon as they've left the kitchen, Danny makes a run for the stairs. He sneaks into his cousins' room, which is full of baseball cards and Star Wars toys, closes the door, and perches on the window seat, which overlooks the swimming pool. Below him, he can see his parents arguing in one corner, while in another, Belle and Carol continue their discussion. Belle is trying to explain that Elaine cannot take care of a household, and this is her problem, and Carol is shaking her head. As for Nick, he has moved out onto the lawn, where he is playing baseball with Greg and Jeff.

Danny can just barely make out his parents' voices. "They arranged this," he hears Elaine saying. "They think Danny's a pain in the ass."

"You know I'd take him if I could," Allen answers.

"I thought you were leading such a model life!"

"There's nothing about my life which would create an unhealthy atmosphere for Danny. I'm just not ready for him yet."

"Good," Elaine says. "He can come live with me."

Danny closes the window. He knows to cover up his tracks. Then he runs back downstairs, through the kitchen, and out the screen door. He runs alongside the pool, past his parents, and toward the woods. Allen catches his eye, and waves. Danny waves back, keeps running.

When Danny first arrived at Nick and Carol's, everything was alien: the extra bed in Greg and Jeff's room which pulled out from under, the coloration of the television set, the spaghetti sauce. They were so indulgent toward him, in his unhappiness, that he wondered if perhaps he had leukemia, and they weren't telling him. And then he realized that he did not have leukemia. He was merely the passive victim of a broken home. For months he had held back his own fear and anger for the sake of his mother. Now she had betrayed him. She *was* unfit. He *had* been taken away, as had she. There was no reason to be good anymore.

What Danny didn't count on was Carol and Nick's expectation that somehow he would change, shape himself to their lives. No child with leukemia would be asked to change. Danny decided to become a child with leukemia—a sick child, a thwarted child, a child to be indulged. Nick and Carol asked him if he wouldn't maybe consider trading places with his grandmother and moving into his cousins' room, which would be fun for all three, like camp. Danny threw his biggest fit ever. They never asked him again. They gave him wearied looks, when he refused to eat, when he demanded to watch what he wanted to watch, when he wouldn't talk to company. They lost patience, and he in turn lost patience: Didn't they understand? He was a victim. And certainly he had only to mention his mother's name, and his own stomach would sink, and Carol's eyes would soften, and suddenly she would become like his grandmother—maternal and embracing. He made himself need her to be maternal and embracing.

The night his mother went to bed forever, Danny learned two things: to be silent was to be crazy, and to be loud was also to be crazy.

It seemed to him that he did not have a choice. He knew no way of living that did not include morose silences and fits of fury. When Carol asked him why he wouldn't just enjoy the life he had, he felt a fierce resistance rise in his chest. He was not going to give himself up.

Now, running from his crazy parents, Danny arrives at a place in the woods—a patch of dry leaves sheltered by an old sycamore—which he has designated his own. Only a few feet away, the neighborhood children are playing Capture the Flag in the cul-de-sac, and he can hear their screams and warnings through the trees. He turns around once, circling his territory, and then he begins. Today he will invent an episode of "The Perfect Brothers Show," the variety show on his personal network. He has several other series in the works, including "Grippo," a detective drama, and "Pierre!" set in the capital city of South Dakota.

He begins. He does all the voices, and makes the sound of applause by driving his tongue against the roof of his mouth. "And now," he says, "for your viewing pleasure, another episode of 'The Perfect Brothers Show'!"

The orchestra plays a fanfare. In another voice, Danny sings:

> *"A perfect night for comedy!*
> *For fun and musicality!*
> *We'll change you!*
> *Rearrange you!*
> *Just you wait and see!*
> *Welcome to The Perfect Brothers Show!"*

He is in the midst of inventing a comic skit, followed by a song from this week's guest star, Loni Anderson, when Jeff—the younger and more persistently good-natured of the brothers—appears from between the trees. "Can I play?" he asks.

Danny, to his own surprise, doesn't throw a fit. "Yes," he says. "We'll do a comedy skit. You're the housewife and I'm Superman."

"I want to be Superman," Jeff says.

"All right, all right." Now Danny begins to give instructions for the skit, but halfway through Jeff interrupts and says, "This is boring. Let's play baseball."

"If you want to play something like *that*," Danny says, "go play Capture the Flag." He throws up his hands in disgust.

"There are girls playing," Jeff says. "Well, if you won't play, I'll play baseball with my dad!"

"Good," says Danny. "Leave me alone."

Jeff runs off toward the house. Part of the way there, he turns once. "You're weird," he says.

Danny ignores him. He is halfway through his skit—playing both parts—when he is interrupted again. This time it is his father. "How are you, old man?" Allen asks. "Want to go to the Paper Palace?"

For a moment Danny's eyes widen, and then he remembers how unhappy he is. "All right," he says.

They take Carol's station wagon, and drive to the Paper Palace, a huge pink cement structure in the middle of an old shopping center. The shopping center is near Danny's old house.

"You've loved the Paper Palace—how long?" Allen asks. "I think you were four the first time I brought you here. You loved it. Remember what I bought you?"

"An origami set and a Richie Rich comic book," Danny says. He rarely gets to the Paper Palace anymore; Carol shops in the more elegant mall near her house.

"When we lived here, all I wanted to do was to get into Carol and Nick's neighborhood. A year ago today. Just think. All I could think about was getting a raise and buying a house. I might have bought the house next door to Carol and Nick's. I wanted you to grow up in that area. All those trees. The fresh air. The great club."

"I am anyhow, I guess," Danny says.

"Don't let it fool you," Allen says. "It all seems so perfect. It all looks so perfect. But soon enough the paint chips, there are corners bitten by the dog, you start sweeping things under the bed. Believe me, under the beds, there's as much dust in Nick and Carol's house as there was in ours."

"Carol has a maid," Danny says.

"Just never trust cleanness. All the bad stuff—the really bad stuff—happens in clean houses, where everything's tidy and nobody says anything more than good morning."

"Our house wasn't like that," Danny says.

Allen looks at him. But now they are in the parking lot of the shopping center, and the colorful promise of the Paper Palace takes both of them over. They rush inside. Danny browses ritualistically at stationery and comic books, reads through the plot synopses in the soap opera magazines, scrupulously notes each misspelling of a character's name. Allen lags behind him. They buy a copy of *Vogue* for Elaine. In front of them in line, a fat, balding man upsets a box of candy on the sales counter as he purchases a copy of *Playgirl*. His effort to avoid attention has backfired, and drawn the complicated looks of all around him. Danny avoids looking at Allen, but Allen's eyes shoot straight to Danny, whose face has a pained, embarrassed expression on it. They do not mention the fat man as they walk out of the store.

Years ago, when Danny was only six or seven, he found a magazine. He was playing in the basement, dressing up in some old clothes of Allen's which he had found in a cardboard box. The magazine was at the bottom of the box. When Elaine came down to check what Danny was up to, she found him sitting on a trunk, examining a series of pictures of young, dazed-looking men posed to simulate various acts of fornication. Elaine grabbed the magazine away from Danny and demanded to know where he'd gotten it. He told her that he had found it, and he pointed to the box.

Elaine looked again at the magazine, and then at the box. She thumbed through the pages, looking at the photographs. Then she put the magazine down on top of the box and wrapped her arms around herself.

"Danny," she said, "for God's sake, don't lie about this. You don't have to. You can tell me the truth. Are you sure that's where you got this thing?"

"Swear to God and hope to die, stick a needle in my eye," Danny said.

"Get upstairs," said Elaine.

"Do you want a Velamint?" Allen asks Danny in the car, as they drive back from the Paper Palace. They are riding down a wide, dark road, lined with sycamores. Danny takes the small blue wafer from his father, without saying anything. He opens the window, sticks his hand out into the breeze.

"You know, Danny, I've been thinking," Allen says. "I know this fantastic place, this school, in New Hampshire. It's great—really innovative—and it's specially for bright, motivated kids like you."

Danny doesn't answer. When Allen turns to look at him, he sees that his son is clutching the armrest so hard his knuckles have turned white, and biting his lip to hold back tears.

"Danny," Allen says. "Danny, what's wrong?"

"I know I've been a problem," Danny says. "But I've decided to change. Today. I've decided to be happy. Please. I'll make them want me to stay."

Allen is alarmed by Danny's panic. "Danny," he says, "this school isn't punishment. It's a great place. You deserve to go there."

"I played with Jeff today!" Danny says. His voice is at its highest register. He is staring at Allen, his face flushed, a look of pure pleading in his eyes.

Allen puts his hand over his mouth and winces. When they reach a stop sign, he turns to Danny and says, as emphatically as he can, "Danny, don't worry, no one's going to *make* you go anywhere. But, Danny, I don't know if I *want* you to stay with Nick and Carol. After fifteen years in that world, I don't know if I want my son to be hurt by it like I was."

"I won't become a stockbroker. I won't sweep the dust under the bed. But, please, don't send me away."

"Danny, I thought you didn't like it here," Allen says.

"I'm not unfit."

They are still at the stop sign. Behind them, a car is honking, urging them to move on. Danny's eyes are brimming with tears.

Allen shakes his head, and reaches for his son.

They go to Carvel's for ice cream. Ahead of them in line a flustered-looking woman buys cones for ten black children who stand in pairs, holding hands. Two of the girls are pulling violently at each other's arms, while a boy whose spiral of soft-serve ice cream has fallen off his cone cries loudly, and demands reparations. Allen orders two chocolate cones with brown bonnets, and he and Danny sit down in chairs with tiny desks attached to them, like the chairs in Danny's elementary school. There are red lines from tears on Danny's face, but he doesn't really cry—at least, he doesn't make any of the crying noises, the heaves and stuttering wails. He picks off the chocolate coating of the brown bonnet and eats it in pieces before even touching the actual ice cream.

"I'm glad you haven't lost your appetite," Allen says.

Danny nods weakly, and continues to eat. The woman marches the ten children out the door, and into a small pink van. "Danny," Allen says, "what can I say? What do you want me to say?"

Danny bites off the bottom of his cone. Half-melted ice cream plops onto the little desk. "Jesus Christ," Allen mutters, and rubs his eyes.

When they get back to the house, Allen joins Nick and Carol under the umbrella on the patio. Elaine is still lying on the chaise, her eyes closed. Danny gets out of the car after his father, walks a circle around the pool, biting his thumbnail, and resumes his position on the diving board. Nearby, Greg and Jeff are again playing catch. "Hey, Danny, want to throw the ball?" Allen shouts. He does not hear Carol hiss her warning, "No!" But Danny neither does nor says anything.

"Danny!" Allen shouts again. "Can you hear me?"

Very slowly Danny hoists himself up, crawls off the diving board and walks back toward the house.

"Oh, Christ," Carol says, taking off her sunglasses. "This is more than I can take."

Now Belle appears at the kitchen door, waving a batter-caked spatula. "What happened?" she asks.

"The same story," Carol says.

"I'll see to him," Allen says. He casts a parting glance at Elaine, and walks into the kitchen. "The same thing happened this morning," Belle tells him as they walk toward Danny's room.

But this time, the door is wide open, instead of slammed shut, and Danny is lying on his back on the bed, his face blank, his eyes tearless.

At first Belle thinks he is sick. "Honey, are you all right?" she asks, feeling his head. "He's cool," she tells Allen.

Allen sits down on the bed and arcs his arms over Danny's stomach. "Danny, what's wrong?" he asks.

Danny turns to look at his father, his face full of a pain too strong for a child to mimic.

"I can't change," he says. "I can't change. I can't change."

*   *   *

In the kitchen, Belle is wrathful. She does not keep her voice down; she does not seem to care that Danny can hear every word she is saying. "I see red when I look at you people," she tells her children. "In my day, people didn't just abandon everything to gratify themselves. In my day, people didn't abandon their children. You're so selfish, all you think about is yourselves."

"What do you want from me?" Allen answers. "What kind of father could I have been? I was living a lie."

"See what I mean?" Belle says. "Selfish. You assume I'm talking about you. But I'm talking about all of you. And you, too, Carol."

"For Christ's sake, Mother, he's not my son!" Carol says. "And he's wrecking my sons' lives. And my life."

Elaine has been fingering her hair. But now she suddenly slams her hand against the table and lets out a little moan. "He really said that?" she says. "Oh, Christ, he really said that."

"I've had it up to here with all of you," Belle announces. "It's unspeakable. I've heard enough."

She turns from them all, as if she has seen enough as well. Allen and Elaine and Nick look down at the table, like ashamed children. But Carol gets up, and walks very deliberately to face her mother. "Now just one minute," she says, her lips twitching with anger. "Just one minute. It's easy for you to just stand there and rant and rave. But I have to live with it, day in and day out, I have to take care of him and put up with his crap. And I have to listen to my kids say, 'What's with that Danny? When's he going away?' Well, maybe I am selfish. I've worked hard to raise my kids well. And now, just because Elaine screws everything up for herself, suddenly I'm expected to bear the brunt of it, take all the punishment. And everything I've been working for is going down the tubes because she can't take care of her own kid! Well, then, I will be selfish. I am selfish. I have had enough of this."

"Now just a minute, Carol," Allen says.

"You take him," Carol says, turning around to confront him. "You take him home, or don't say a word to me. There's not one word you have a right to say to me."

"Damn it!" Allen says. "Doesn't anybody understand? I'm doing my best."

"You've had two months," Nick says.

Belle, her arms wrapped around her waist, begins to cry softly. Sitting at the table, Elaine cries as well, though more loudly, and with less decorum.

Then, with a small click, the door to Danny's bedroom opens, and he walks into the kitchen. Allen and Nick stand up, nearly knocking their chairs over in the process. "Danny!" Carol says. Her voice edges on panic. "Are you all right?"

"Yes, thank you," Danny says.

Elaine lifts her head from the table. "Danny," she says. "Danny, I—" She moves her lips, struggling to form words. But nothing comes out. Danny looks down at her, his eyes full of a frightening, adult pity. Then he turns away and walks outside.

Everyone jumps up at once to follow him. But Allen holds up his hand. "I'll go," he says. He scrambles out the door, and after Danny, who is marching past the swimming pool, toward the patch of woods where he likes to play. When he gets there, he stops and waits, his back to his father.

"Danny," Allen says, coming up behind him. "You heard everything. I don't know what to say. I wish I did."

Danny has his arms crossed tightly over his chest. "I've thought about it," he says. "I've decided."

"What?" Allen says.

"About the school," Danny says. "I've decided I'll go."

*   *   *

A few days later, Danny boards the train which snakes along the Jersey coast to New York. He is riding to visit his father. An old couple is sitting across the way from him, a gnarled little man and his taller, white-haired wife, her white-gloved hands clasped calmly around each other. Like Danny, the couple is not reading the paper, but looking out the green-tinted windows at yellow grass, small shops, warehouses.

"You'd better get your things together," the husband says. "We're almost there."

"No," the wife says. "We don't want South Amboy. We want Perth Amboy." The husband shakes his head no. "South Amboy. I'm sure she said South Amboy."

The wife is quiet for a few seconds, until the conductor shouts, "South Amboy, South Amboy next!" Now she cannot control herself. "I'm *sure* it's Perth Amboy," she says. The husband is buttoning his jacket, reaching for his hat. "Will you listen to me for once?" he says. "Its South Amboy." The wife shakes her head. "I'm sure," she says. "I'm sure."

Gradually, and then with a sudden grind, the train comes to a halt. The husband lumbers down the aisle, knocking past Danny, shaking his head. "I'm getting off," he says. "Are you coming?" The wife stands, hesitates, sits down. "It's not this stop," she says. He makes a violent motion with his hands, and walks out the door, onto the station platform. She stands to follow him, but the doors close suddenly. His fist appears, as if disembodied, rapping on the window. Then the train is moving again.

For a moment, she just stands there, shocked. Then the train's lurching forces her to sit down. A look comes over her face first of indignation, then of fear and confusion, then finally, of weariness—with her husband, with the train, with their lives which will go on like this. She bends over and pulls herself into the corner of her seat, as if trying to make herself as small as possible, and picks at a loose thread of her dress with one of her white-gloved hands.

Then she comes to consciousness. She realizes that she is not alone on the train. Her eyes narrow, and focus on Danny. Late afternoon, almost dark. He is singing a song about comedy and fun and musicality. He tells her it's going to be a perfect night.

Family Dancing

Although just barely—without *laudes*, without distinction, and from an academy which is third-rate at best—Suzanne Kaplan's son, Seth, has managed to graduate from prep school, and Suzanne is having a party to celebrate. The party is also a celebration of Suzanne's own "graduation into life"—her thirty pounds thinner body, her new house, and her new marriage to Bruce Kaplan, who works in real estate. Of course, Suzanne has been planning for the party to take place outdoors, since Seth's graduation coincides with the brief, fragile season of wisteria, and the pool looks gorgeous in sunlight. Unfortunately, it's been raining every day for a week now, and Suzanne's spent a lot of time by her kitchen window, reminding herself that she should still be counting her blessings.

"It's a drowning spring," Suzanne's mother, Pearl, told her the day before the party. "Don't count on outdoors. Move everything inside to the nice family room." But Suzanne was optimistic, and sure enough, this morning, the morning of the party, the sun has risen brilliantly, and the wet grass promises to be dry by noon. In her new bathrobe, she stands in the living room, and watches Bruce drive his power mower. His children, Linda and Sam, are playing a game she doesn't recognize, and she raps on the window to get their attention.

They stop jarringly when they hear her, as if they have been caught in the act of defacing something. They look at her; it is a look she calls the "wicked witch" look, because her own daughter, Lynnette, used to give it before running off to her room, screaming, "You're a witch." Suzanne isn't privy to the secrets of Linda and Sam's lives; they are polite, but keep their distance. Of course, to them, she is the new, alien thing.

She pushes open the sliding glass door and walks out onto the patio. "What are you playing?" she asks, but even now her voice trembles. She knows they can see right through her nonchalance.

"Nothing," Linda says. "Come on, Sam."

Her brother gives Suzanne a helpless glance, and then they are off, to another part of the yard.

The yard is spacious, green. To the north is a huge meadow where cows might still graze, if there were any more cows in this part of the world. The part of the Bronx where Suzanne grew up is now a vast region of housing projects, but when she was a child, living in a two-family house, there were still wild patches of countryside, and farmhouses, and even some farmers. These days, when she drives to visit her mother, she stops sometimes. Off the highway there are occasional plots of what used to be farmland, grown over with wild grasses and gnarled trees. The farmhouses which are left are rotting, and only squatters inhabit them.

Of course, Suzanne doesn't live in the Bronx anymore. She has moved "up" in the world, as her mother might put it, though "up" has always seemed the wrong word: it's struck her as a more lateral movement. Now, in her mother's mind, she is on some sort of summit, having recovered beautifully from the horrific fall of her divorce. In her mother's mind, Suzanne is in the clouds. She herself feels more on earth than ever before, but she is happy to know (if nothing else) that she has perhaps finally arrived somewhere.

It has been just over a year since Suzanne's first husband, Herb, informed her that he was in love with a lawyer from his office. At that time they were living in Rockville Centre, in the third of what would probably have been four houses, and Suzanne was fat. Herb, she remembers, had recently gotten a substantial salary hike, Lynnette had finally moved to Manhattan, they were out of eggs, and the dishwasher was broken. When Herb said he wanted to talk to her after dinner, she hoped he was going to suggest that they now move to a posher suburb, with larger lawns, for he had been skillfully avoiding the subject of a move for months. Instead, his announcement confirmed all the suspicions Suzanne had been trying to talk herself out of since the second house. The inevitability of it was something like relief to her, but that did not make it easier to bear.

Herb said he wouldn't leave Suzanne. He said he believed in responsibility and commitment. But he would not give up his lover, either; everything must be aboveboard. "What is it?" Suzanne asked him that night. "Is it that I'm fat and depressed and a bitch? Is that all?"

"It is simply that I'm in love with someone else," Herb said. She supposed he meant these words to be soothing, because they included no attacks, and she was amazed that he could not know how much they pierced her. Still, she wanted him to stay.

"Fine," he said. "But two nights a week—probably Tuesday and Thursday—and some weekends, I'll stay in the city with Selena."

The first Tuesday night he was gone she thought she would go mad. She was so angry at Herb that she seriously feared losing control, doing him some terrible violence, and she resolved to tell him the next evening that he must move out. She resented even more his insinuating trick of making her kick him out when it was he who wanted to leave. Up until that night, in the recesses of Suzanne's self-hatred, there had rested an incurable sense of being blessed, an assurance that there awaited her some pleasurable vengeance against all this suffering, which gave her pain an anticipatory edge. Now Herb had shaved that edge clean off. She knew there was no guardian angel to make sure he got what he deserved, or suddenly revitalize his love for her. And she wished that Herb had simply, swiftly died in his car on the Long Island Expressway, rather than do what she most dreaded, and confirm every terrible charge she had made against herself. Wednesday night, when he came home, she told him not to bother to come back.

The human body, Suzanne remembers, seemed at that time impossibly ugly; aging, mortality, its capacity to fall apart were all part of a sick joke, played by a vengeful God. She did not want to kill herself. She wanted to last forever, rotting, like Miss Havisham in *Great Expectations*, or like the farmhouses in the Bronx. She wanted to always remind the human race of its talent for shame and ruin. When she woke up each morning, however, some irritating instinct for survival and pleasure nagged at her. She wished it would go away, but it would not, and finally she got out of bed, and washed her hair, and walked into the living room to survey the damage. Lynnette was in New York, Seth at school. The thought of continuing to live in this room made her nauseous, and for a moment, the emptiness and the loneliness of her house threatened to drive her back into bed. But this was her lot, and whether she liked it or not, she must make something—perhaps the best—out of it. And so she cleaned up. And, trembling a little, went to the grocery store and bought herself some food to make for dinner. The television set pulled her through the first week. The second week she tried to curb how much she watched, knowing that "Saturday Night Live," like an addictive drug, might lose its effectiveness if she overdosed. The third week she signed up to join a depression therapy group.

Herb and the lawyer broke up three months after he moved into her apartment, but he decided to stay in Manhattan and get his own place. At that time, Suzanne had just met Bruce, whose own wife had left him a few weeks before. Her life seemed quite suddenly enormous with possibility, and the news of Herb's break-up filled her with a kind of vengeful glee. Of course, she told herself, if he asked her, she would not take him back, not now. But he has never asked her. Instead he says he is extraordinarily happy for Suzanne, absolutely delighted that things worked out so well for her. He expresses no resentment, no jealousy, only a kind of relief, as if a burden of guilt has been lifted from him. When they had lunch together last week, to discuss Seth's graduation, Suzanne tried to enjoy the fact that she, the loser, the victim, had come out on top in the end—better than ever before. But Herb seemed to enjoy Suzanne's happiness as much as she did, and she left the restaurant feeling choked inside. She was miserable because Herb was not miserable, yet her own victor-status demanded that she not be concerned with that. Still, she raged at his uncanny talent for happiness.

Herb says that he wants to be Suzanne's friend. He speaks to her in intimate tones unheard through the long course of their marriage. "It's amazing," he told her at last week's lunch, "but I'm beginning to realize why it bugged me so much when you used to talk about getting a new house. It wasn't just that I was planning to ask you to let me out of the marriage. It was the thought that the next house was going to be the last house, the house we'd probably die in. We were rich enough that we could finally afford the best, and that meant there was nowhere left to go. I felt like my life was over. But now, I don't know about you, Suzanne, but I've had to reassess my whole value system. I'm seeing a counselor. I'm realizing all the things I did wrong as a father. Really, for both of us, things are just beginning."

Suzanne looked at him and thought, How dare he speak like this, now? It was as if he believed the old Suzanne—the woman who would have been crushed by such a statement—had simply ceased to exist. This was a new model, in whom he could confide the ugly truth about his shrewish, fat wife and their wretched life together. And though on good days, Suzanne would almost agree with Herb— she imagines that she has been reincarnated, that the old Suzanne lived in a different age, and had a life utterly distinct from her own— on bad days, it is as if almost no time has passed; as if her marriage to Bruce, her weight loss, her new house are all simply part of a dream from which she will awaken, to find herself in the old bed, the old house. Those days, she feels like an earthquake survivor who carries around the rubble of her home in a bag, refusing to let go her buried children.

Now, coming back in from the porch, Suzanne looks at the clock. It is already eleven, and Seth is still asleep; sunlight is leaking through the crack in the guest-room door. Suzanne stands before her son's room and knocks cautiously, but she gets no answer.

"Seth," she says.

There is a sound of thrashing inside the room.

"Seth, wake up," Suzanne says. "It's already eleven."

"All right, all right," he mumbles, "Give me ten minutes."

"Seth, it's your party, you've got to get up."

"Leave me alone!" he shouts. Suzanne smiles, knowing that if she gets him angry enough, he'll be too riled to sleep. It's what she calls a mother's secret.

Now she pushes the door open, and the leak of sunlight engulfs her. Seth is splayed diagonally across the double bed, in his underwear, wrapped in a tangle of sheets and blankets.

"Come on," Suzanne says in a singsong voice. "It's time to get up!"

He sits up in bed quite suddenly and stares at her, furious. "Do you know how much sleep I got during finals week?" he asks.

"How much?"

"Maybe ten minutes. Can't I make up for it now?"

"Do you still want to?" Suzanne asks. Seth looks at her with the confused expression he often had as a child, when he would come into the kitchen in the morning, bleary-eyed, and slurp down the sweet milk in which he had drowned his cereal.

"Happy party day," she says, and walks out of the room.

But when Suzanne gets downstairs, she finds that her quiet kitchen is suddenly ablaze with activity. The caterers have arrived—a crew of large, stubbornly bourgeois black women, all related to each other in obscure ways, who have recently been earning an impressive reputation in this part of Long Island. The women are dressed in various combinations of black-and-white polyester which look to Suzanne like military uniforms, and seem to indicate a complicated hierarchy. Suzanne's mother, Pearl, has also arrived; she is now talking to a particularly large woman of middle age whose black hostess dress (without a strip of white) signals supreme authority. They are going over the hors d'oeuvres.

"Curried lobster puffs, sausage rolls au gratin, sesame chicken wings, cheese-filled mini-croissants, Polynesian turkey meatballs, baked brie. Oh, and the chopped liver," the woman says.

"Yes," Pearl says, "and tell me, Mrs. Ferguson, is the chopped liver in a shape, or what?"

"It's in the shape of a heart," Mrs. Ferguson says.

"A heart!" says Pearl.

Mrs. Ferguson folds her arms. "What's wrong with a heart?" she asks.

"Oh, nothing, nothing," Pearl says. "Why, look, here comes my daughter the hostess."

"Hello," Suzanne says, grasping Mrs. Ferguson's hand. "I'm glad to see my mother's taken charge already. I hope things are going all right."

"Things are fine but you don't have a pastry tube!" shouts a tiny old woman in a chef's hat. "What you mean not having a pastry tube?"

"No pastry tube!" Suzanne says. "Are you sure? I've just moved in and I don't know what we have."

"I'll have to send the girl back in the van," the old woman says, shaking her head with annoyance. "We'll be late because of this. Gloria!"

A teenaged girl rushes over to consult with the old woman in the chef's hat. In the meantime, all around Suzanne, other girls go to work—rolling up the sausages, filling the mini-croissants, icing the cake.

Into the kitchen now strides Suzanne's daughter, Lynnette, who is twenty-three and a secretary in Manhattan. She is not a person who can slip into rooms quietly, and so everyone has turned to notice her. With Lynnette is her best friend and roommate, John, a tall, emaciated young man with caved-in cheeks. "Hello, Mother," Lynnette says. "I see we're just in time to get in the way."

Lynnette is wearing a black dress which looks like several lace slips sewn together. She has a flower in her hair, a wild pink geranium, and her face is streaked with purple and blue make-up. If she weren't so fat, Suzanne thinks, she would look half decent, but Suzanne knows that Lynnette has chosen the dress specifically because it most explicitly reveals the bulges of her abdomen and buttocks. John is also dressed outrageously, in a purple suit and flaming yellow bow tie.

"Hello, Mrs. Kaplan," he says, the way (Suzanne thinks) he always says hello to her—grudgingly, and with an undertone of hatred. Suzanne is sure resentful Lynnette has filled his head with stories about her—the wicked witch—and as recompense, she is excessively cordial whenever she sees John. "Hello," she says, taking his hand. "I'm so happy to see you again. Just wait till you taste that baked brie, it's fabulous."

Nearby two of the girls who are rolling sausage rolls have stopped their work and are staring at John and Lynnette. They keep staring until Mrs. Ferguson slaps them simultaneously on the backs of their necks and tells them to get back to work.

"Suzanne!" Pearl whispers fiercely, grabbing her daughter's hand from behind. "The chopped liver in a heart shape! Those *shvartzeh* caterers put the chopped liver in a heart shape!"

Now, puffing, Bruce enters the kitchen. He is wearing knee-length Bermuda shorts, and his skin has reddened to the shade of his hair from the ordeal of mowing. "Everything under control?" he asks, and all the women—even Suzanne—instinctively back away from his sweating male presence, as if it might contaminate the food.

Bruce looks around himself shyly, and wraps his arms around his stomach, as if he imagines he is naked in his own kitchen. "Maybe I should just get out of the way," he says.

"That might be a good idea," Suzanne says. She feels a certain tenderness toward him right now, as if he were a lost child. And yet she knows that tenderness is simply another cover for her true feeling toward him—the feeling of disappointment. They met in the depression therapy group. Bruce's wife had up and left him and their children to go off to California with a twenty-two-year-old auto mechanic. Suzanne and Bruce fed each other's misery and self-pity for a time, and then, drunk one night, they made love on the spur of the moment. As Suzanne tells it, Bruce made her feel attractive, like a real woman, for the first time in twenty years, she all but stopped eating, and the next week they eloped to Las Vegas.

*   *   *

In the corner of the kitchen, Lynnette watches her mother watch Bruce, and smirks. She actually thinks, I am smirking. Everything about the house, the caterers, the party, confirms her worst suspicions. She has no doubt but that her mother is very happy with all of it, that every petit-bourgeois value she has ascribed to Suzanne is pathetically, miserably accurate.

Though she would never admit it, Lynnette has been looking forward to this party with real ferocity. She is a loudmouthed girl whom most people find unpleasant, and she would tell you in a minute how much she hates herself. Her loyalties to others, though few, are fierce. John, for instance: She likes him more than anyone she knows her own age. John is gay, and his parents, who live only a few miles from Suzanne, will hardly speak to him. She must remember that he has probably been hurt more by this world even than she has, and she looks to him sympathetically, as his friend. She hopes her look gives him strength.

Lynnette's other great loyalty is to her father. All through her childhood the two of them cultivated a relationship which almost consciously excluded Suzanne and Seth. She will always remember the trips to the park that she and Herb took after dinner, and how up until she was thirteen or so, and too big to fit, he would push her on the swing, higher and higher, until the sky seemed to tilt wildly, and she was flying. She was a heavy little girl, but that never seemed to deter him. He picked her up effortlessly as if he were a ballet dancer, and she his prima ballerina. "You're my favorite partner," he'd tell her as he pushed her on the swing. "Your favorite?" she'd say. "Better than Mommy?" "Yes, better than Mommy," he'd say. "Someday we'll dance under the stars."

Years later, he fulfilled that promise. He had just moved in with Selena, and there was so much love between them that they seemed to need Lynnette to soak up the excess. They took her to the ballet, to see

Peter Martins and Suzanne Farrell, and afterward for a spontaneous ride on the Staten Island Ferry, and there, under starlight, Herb took his daughter in his arms and danced with her while Selena sat by and beamed. Their clumsy pas de deux had no musical accompaniment, but Lynnette didn't care. She felt as if Herb's new life with Selena was her new life, as if his optimism might actually prove contagious. That night the world had seemed endless in its possibilities.

Of course, soon afterward, Herb and Selena broke up. Herb's been seeing another woman recently, an architect named Miriam, but Lynnette knows the excitement isn't there. Theirs is the moderate, efficient love of older people who have led complicated lives. Though she misses Selena, she makes every effort to be cordial to Miriam, and wants to be her friend. Above all else, she is determined not to be perceived as the jealous daughter.

Lynnette looks at her mother, who is discussing something with Mrs. Ferguson. Their relationship has never been easy, but only recently has Lynnette figured out why Suzanne resents her so much. It is because Lynnette has managed to retain what Suzanne has irretrievably lost: She has managed to retain Herb's love. Across from her Bruce stands in a corner, cowed by so much activity: small, plump, meek Bruce. Suzanne is watching Bruce as well. For a brief second, mother's and daughter's stares meet. In recent conversations, Lynnette has heard Suzanne refer to Herb still as her husband, and not even catch the slip.

They are both thinking the same thing, Lynnette knows. They are both thinking what a handsome, protective, intelligent man Herb is. The only difference is that what Suzanne thinks with a pang of regret and terror, Lynnette thinks—smirkingly—with a taste of triumph.

John—his purple suit turning a strange shade of mauve in the shadows—is flirting with one of the girls who will serve lunch.

"What's Irish and sits on your porch?" he asks, and the girl giggles, shrugging her shoulders.

"Patio furniture," John says. The girl, who is not more than sixteen, now starts to laugh uncontrollably. It's clear she doesn't want to be laughing; she keeps looking over her shoulder, to see if Mrs. Ferguson is watching her. And indeed, Mrs. Ferguson occasionally throws sidelong glances at the girl, though it's obvious she doesn't intend to do anything now. She is waiting until after the party, when she can punish in private.

Now John is telling an obscene story about Michael Jackson and the baby tiger on his record cover. Suzanne listens with some distaste. She does not trust John for a second. And not because he is gay, either. That has nothing to do with it. What annoys Suzanne about John is his intolerance. She remembers the day he and Lynnette first met Bruce, and Bruce had the mistaken impression that John was Lynnette's boyfriend. He took him outside after dinner and walked him around the garden and told John that he had a future with Bruce's real estate firm, if he wanted one. It seemed like the proper thing to do. Suzanne blushes at the thought of Bruce's naïveté, but when she remembers overhearing Lynnette and John laughing uncontrollably, and mocking her husband, her embarrassment turns to anger and impatience.

Lynnette is going through the cereal drawer. "Mom?" she asks. "Does Seth eat anything but Sugar Pops these days?"

"Corn Bran," Suzanne says.

"I'm now in the room, so please don't talk about me in the third person," Seth says. He is standing in the doorway, wearing his droopy bathrobe. "Yes," he says. "It's me."

Pearl puts down the paper graduation cap she is constructing, and rushes over to hug her grandson. "Sethela," she says, "you're so big now. A real graduation boy." She kisses him.

Over the heads of Lynnette, Suzanne, and Pearl, John and Seth—
the tallest people in the room by five or six inches—nod to each other.

"Seth," Suzanne says, "you got a card from Concetta." She hands
him an envelope postmarked Jamaica. "Ex-maid," Lynnette whispers to John.

Seth smiles, and tears open the envelope. The card has a
picture of a happy white-faced boy holding some flowers on it. He
opens it, wrinkles his brow, and begins to read, silently moving
his lips.

Now he looks up, smiles, and reads aloud: "God Bless you on your
birthday." He looks again at the card, and begins to study the second
line.

The tiny woman in the chef's hat is whispering furiously to Mrs.
Ferguson. After nodding a few times, Mrs. Ferguson walks out of the
kitchen, beckoning Suzanne to follow her. Suzanne goes, sheepish,
expecting punishment.

"She wants all of you out of the kitchen," Mrs. Ferguson says.
"Now."

"O.K.," Suzanne says. She goes back into the kitchen. "Come on,
kids," she says. "The caterers have work to do."

Seth is on the fourth line of the card.

All through his childhood, Seth was a problem. Suzanne and Herb
chastised him—for laziness, for addiction to television, even for
occasional outbursts of hyperactive violence, during which he might
bounce on their bed until the bedboard broke. He was a difficult
child, and to compensate for the impenetrable closeness shared by
Herb and Lynnette, Suzanne contrived an affection for him which
had less to do with maternal instinct than with a mournful thirst for
justice. Over the years, this bond of weakness has taken on enormous strength. Suzanne loves this difficult child, for reasons she

cannot, and would not, want to articulate. And up until he was four-teen, Seth loved her as much in return.

But Suzanne was a coward. When Herb almost casually called Seth stupid, she said nothing. When Herb doled out punishment after Seth got bad grades, she said nothing. Suzanne never thought to have him tested for a learning disability because above all else, she feared annoying Herb. When Seth's guidance counselor told Suzanne of his dyslexia—adding crisply that she was shocked at how long it had gone unnoticed—Suzanne burst into a fit of tears so violent that the nurse had to be called.

Herb decided that Seth should go to boarding school. He had been told of a place in Vermont that specialized in cases such as his. Before he broke the news, he told Seth he could have anything he wanted, and the boy's face immediately darkened with suspicion, for he was a child who often wanted things fiercely, and rarely got them. After a few seconds Seth muttered that he might like a television for the back of the car. When Herb told him about the boarding school, Seth's mouth opened, and water screened his eyes. Suzanne had to leave the room.

Seth went to boarding school. At first he cried all the time, and begged to go home, but after a few weeks he adjusted to his new life. Since then, he has worked consistently and diligently to overcome the learning disability. He has won the praise and affection of his teachers. And he has told Suzanne that the school has come to seem to him more of a home than any place he's ever lived.

It occurs to Suzanne, from time to time, that she has lost Seth. Not the way mothers are supposed to lose their children—by loving them too much or hurting them or both—but the way one might lose a safety pin or a set of keys. Simply by distraction, by neglect. She might find him again soon, just as accidentally. Their lives might change, and they might come to need each other again. As it stands, she doesn't worry about it because she is nearly as impressed by Seth's capacity for recovery as she is by her own.

There has been some debate within the family as to what Herb and Suzanne should give Seth as his graduation gift. Herb wanted to buy him a car, but Suzanne doesn't trust Seth's driving. She thought of a stereo system. Then Herb learned from Lynnette that what Seth really wanted was a sewing machine. He had developed an interest in fashion design, Seth had told Lynnette, and was even thinking about taking some courses at Parson's in the fall. When Herb told Suzanne, she said, "I give up." She was really surprised to find out that Seth was confiding things in Lynnette instead of her. Bruce was also surprised, but for a different reason. "Well," he said, "I suppose if that's what he really wants, it's all right." But everyone is still a little anxious about the gift. It does not seem quite the right thing for a boy graduating from prep school (even though the model Herb chose is state-of-the-art, with computerized controls). And Suzanne wonders how Seth will react. After all, he has never said a word to her about clothes design, or Parson's, or wanting a sewing machine. He has only spoken to Lynnette. How will he feel when he receives the present, and sees that his private ambitions have become part of a public gesture?

The guests begin to arrive around two. There is no sign of the morning's chaos; flowers have been placed strategically around the patio, and the youngest of the caterers' girls are standing in clean white aprons, holding trays of hot hors d'oeuvres, at the four corners. The first guests to arrive are a couple named Barlow, who live about thirty feet away, but have nonetheless driven over. They greet Suzanne and Bruce warmly, smile, comment on the beautiful day, the beautiful wisteria, the beautiful pool. Suzanne accepts their gifts from Mrs. Barlow, while Bruce sternly shakes hands with Mr. Barlow.

"He looks better in a suit," John says to Lynnette. The two of them are sitting on the diving board of the pool, far enough away from the patio that they can comment on the guests without being overheard. "Some people do, you know. Look incredibly silly until they put on a suit. Your stepfather looks quite dapper now, actually. He looks like someone to be reckoned with."

Lynnette smiles, watching her mother crumple in deference to a second couple. "He's worth a few good laughs," she says. "Bruce can tell good jokes. Mannish ones."

John has twisted his legs one around the other, as if they were pieces of pipe cleaner. "I see there's a kiddie table," he says.

"There is. For once, Seth won't have to sit there."

"When I was a kid," John says, "I hated kiddie tables. Sometimes I refused to eat at all if it meant sitting with babies."

"Well, don't worry. Mom didn't have us at the kiddie table, but close enough. We were supposed to eat at the young adult table, with some of my cousins and these people from Queens. But I switched the placecards. Now we're sitting with Daddy and Miriam and Seth."

"Does your mother know you switched the cards?" John asks.

Lynnette smiles. "She'll find out," she says.

"Seth's disappeared again," John says, looking once again toward the house. "I hope we get a chance to talk. It's so strange seeing him in this context."

"Well, he'll be in New York soon. Then we'll see a lot of him, I'm sure. Still, I'd just love to drop it casually to Mom. You know. Seth and John are friends, Mom. They go to this club on Avenue A . . . you probably haven't heard of it. She'd die."

"Don't do anything cruel, Lynnette," John says.

She looks at him, surprised. "What does that mean?" she asks.

"I'm serious. I'm sorry to have to be so blunt, but it bothers me, all of this aggression toward your mother. Switching the placecards and all. The point is not to be pointlessly cruel. The point is different."

"I'm not being pointlessly cruel," Lynnette says. "I'm talking self-preservation. There was no way in hell I was eating lunch with my cousins after all this time."

John looks at the diving board, the still pool below. "Perhaps we should go socialize," he says.

"What is your problem today?" Lynnette says. "Angry one minute, the next everything is just hunky-dory."

"Look, I said what I had to say. Let's go socialize. A lot of people are arriving."

He stands up, brushing some leaves from his lap, and offers Lynnette his hand. "Shall we?" he says.

"All right," she says. She gets up and takes his arm, and they promenade up the grassy slope of the lawn to the patio.

"Oh, Lynnette," Suzanne says once they're in hearing range, "you're just in time to see the Friedlanders. You remember Steve and Emily Friedlander, don't you?"

"Yes, of course," Lynnette says. "I babysat for you in junior high."

"I remember. I do," Mrs. Friedlander says, and shakes Lynnette's hand.

"And this is Lynnette's roommate, John Bachman," Suzanne says.

"I work in publishing," John says, in response to Mr. Friedlander's query.

"Not much money there, is there?" Mr. Friedlander says. "But I suppose someone's got to do it. Emily and I are avid readers. What's the company?"

John names it. "Steve," Emily says, "don't we own that?" She laughs.

"Champagne cocktail," announces one of the young girls with the trays. "Fish mousse," says another. "Mini egg rolls," says another.

Lynnette and John head for the champagne cocktails. They take two each. Suzanne takes one, and drinks it quickly and subtly. Only Bruce says no. He doesn't drink. Someone runs inside to get him some sparkling cider.

In the foyer, the graduation gifts pile up—silver ribbons and designer wrapping papers and huge, ornate bows which glitter in the sunlight.

Seth finally makes it outdoors around three, still looking rumpled, though he's wearing a new pressed suit. Almost immediately he is engulfed by a circle of grandmothers and aunts and great aunts, arrived by taxi from Brooklyn, the Bronx, Yonkers. "Sethela," Pearl says proudly, "you look handsome as a man. How old are you?"

"Almost eighteen," Seth says. Over the heads of these small women he exchanges a glance and a nod with John, who motions with his eyes toward the pool house. Seth watches his friend whisper goodbye to Lynnette, and make his way down the grassy slope to the pool.

"So what are your plans?" Pearl asks. "Tell us all, tell us your plans, you great big graduation man, you."

Suzanne sees Seth talking from the kiddie table, where she is setting up paper plates and special placemats. Bruce's children, Linda and Sam, will sit at the kiddie table, along with two babies, some pubescent nieces, and the seventeen-year-old son of Concetta, the ex-maid. Suzanne can see Linda and Sam, standing glumly on the porch, surveying this party full of strangers. She thinks they are menacing children. She feels a little tipsy after two drinks, and thinks she will have more.

And there, across the porch, is Lynnette, who, in the midst of looking for John, has been swept up by a stronger urge to find her father. Discovering he hasn't arrived, she has sat down and decided to analyze her mother, who is having another drink. Her prognosis: Things are turning over on Suzanne (a turnover which will be completed when she sees the switched placecards). And then Lynnette remembers what John has said, and feels a stab of guilt. It is not her fault, she tells herself, if Suzanne is still in love with Herb, if Bruce is a weak, inferior person. Perhaps there is something wrong with her taking such pleasure in her mother's sad predicament. And yet she takes pleasure in so few things, and if she tells no one, and does nothing to make things worse for Suzanne than Suzanne has already made them for herself, who can fault her? In the long run, Lynnette decides, she is doing her mother a favor by switching the placecards, saving her from the pain of sitting with Herb and Miriam, who are genuinely in love, and would only make Suzanne envious and unhappy.

Where is John? He has disappeared somewhere. Seth is still surrounded by the circle of old women. Her mother is drinking, laughing, chatting. Bruce holds his wife's hand with a kind of tentativeness—the hold of a man who isn't sure what he's clinging to.

No one—not even Lynnette—notices when Seth slips away from his relatives, and makes his way toward the pool house.

Suzanne is standing in the kitchen, holding on to the counter so hard her knuckles are turning white as the marble. She is biting her lower lip and she is fighting back a wave of nausea. Because suddenly, inexplicably, standing with her husband, she felt as alone and bereft as the first day she got out of bed after Herb's departure and stood in the living room on her wobbly legs and cried. There is no need for this, she tells herself. She is in a new house, she is a new person, and she is surrounded by friends and relations, she is having a party. Yet none of it seems real to her. Why now, when she has no time to control it, must the pain return?

She breathes deeply, counts her breaths. Next to her on the counter is a half-empty martini. Without thinking she gulps the drink down, before noticing that someone has extinguished a cigarette butt in it. A pleasant warmth seeps through her, and seems to numb her. She wants desperately to disappear, to watch television, to go to the grocery store. But she cannot, she must not.

And strengthened—at least for the moment—by her drink, she goes back outside.

Suzanne knows Herb has arrived when she gets outside because his name hums in the background, on the lips of all the guests. He is wearing a black-striped suit and a red tie, and he is standing with a pretty blond woman in her thirties who is wearing a white dress: Miriam. Herb has spoken of her, over lunch. They may be married in the spring.

"Daddy, Daddy!" Lynnette shouts, abandoning her search for John and Seth. And she runs from where she is sitting to where he stands, nearly knocking Suzanne over in the process.

"Hi, baby doll," Herb says, sweeping heavy Lynnette up in his arms, clear into the air, as if she is weightless. Miriam stands next to him, her hands crossed over her stomach, holding a small gift. She is the kind of woman who knows how to stand and look comfortable while she is waiting to be introduced, while she is being assessed.

"Hello, Miriam," Lynnette says. "I'm glad you could come." And she whispers something to Herb which no one can catch.

"Hello, Herb," Suzanne says, walking to greet him. If she didn't know about Miriam, she could say something sultry, like, "Who's your friend?" Because she is drunk, she has no idea how she actually sounds.

"You're looking radiant as usual," Herb says. Miriam smiles.

"Oh, Miriam," Herb says, suddenly remembering his companion. "Suzanne, this is Miriam. Miriam, Suzanne."

"Hello, Suzanne," Miriam says. "Herb's told me so much about you." She reaches out her hand, graciously.

"Likewise," Suzanne says.

"Hello, Herb!" A small man suddenly appears by Suzanne's side, and shakes Herb's hand. "Good to see you, buddy," he says. Suzanne looks at the man, a little puzzled, and then she remembers that he is her husband.

"I'll leave you all to talk," Suzanne says. "A hostess's duties call." And she slips off to the kitchen. Suzanne does not usually drink much, and when she does, it's for a reason. On those rare occasions— like today—the power of alcohol impresses her tremendously, and she wants to recommend it, like a wonder drug. She wants to do commercials advertising its effectiveness. Perhaps she can tell Mrs. Ferguson. It is amazing what this stuff can do, she might say. We are all chemicals, after all. And suddenly, her body feels as if it is nothing but chemicals—entirely mechanical, a vat of interaction, immune.

The caterers are carving several legs of lamb. "We're ready to serve if you are, ma'am," shouts the old lady in the chef's hat.

"Oh, I'm ready," Suzanne says. "I'm ready for anything."

She is only surprised, in fact, when she sees her name on a place-card at a table with her cousins from Queens. She remembers arranging things differently. No matter. The Queens cousins can be fun. Anyone can be fun as long as she looks at them, listens to them the right way.

Just as the appetizer is served, Seth and John reappear, somewhat out of breath.

"Where were you?" Lynnette asks.

"We took a walk," John says, and they sit down at the table, with Herb.

"Was it fun?" Herb asks.

"Oh, yes," Seth says. "Quite fun. Hello, Miriam."

From behind them, at another table, Suzanne raises a glass of wine and says, "*Mazel tov*, everybody." Safely ensconced between Herb and John, Lynnette doesn't even smile.

"Suzanne," Bruce says, sitting down next to her. "Suzanne, are you all right? Your eyes are all red."

By dusk, the tables have been cleared.

The caterers are cleaning up the kitchen, to the hum of the dish-washer. The old lady in the chef's hat, once so irritable, is sitting in a corner, polishing a copper skillet and humming "God Bless the Child." Near the diving board, Suzanne watches purple blotches of cloud move and crash against one another. She is dimly aware that somewhere behind her people are talking, relatives mostly. (The Barlows and the Friedlanders left hours ago.) It is hard for her to identify any one voice. Yet she does not feel weak. In some perverse way, she feels strong—strong enough to bulldoze her way through dinner, to keep Myra from talking the whole time about dentistry. Once again, she has gotten past despair. She only wonders how long it will be until the next bout, and if the gulf will have widened.

A roar of laughter is rising above the patio, and a voice—John's voice—says, "Come on, please, dance with me, please." Suzanne gets up and stumbles toward the house, to see what's causing the commo-tion. It seems that Seth has put a dance tape on the stereo—one he made for a party at school—and a disco song with lyrics in German is blasting out the family room windows. The person John is trying to entice into dancing with him is Pearl, and she is shaking her head, no, no, and throwing back her neck, laughing as he reaches out his hands to her and implores her.

"Come on, Pearl," an uncle says. "You used to love to dance with the young men." Yes, the family roars. Dance. And quite suddenly she relents, a smile widening on her face.

Pearl dances with amazing energy. She kicks up her heels, and her sisters and cousins and grandchildren—gathered in a circle—applaud loudly, and cheer her on. Even Seth jumps and whoops with glee. Lynnette sits with Miriam and Herb outside the circle, at a small patio table. They observe this spectacle with polite smiles on their faces, like tourists who watch a native dance and wish they, too, could be primitive and join in. Lynnette gazes at Miriam, whose face is a model of perfect composure. What a contrast, she thinks, to her mother's freak show of a party; how good it feels to be in the company of kind and well-mannered Miriam. Lynnette cannot help but smile, and move her hand toward Miriam's, which lifts slightly off the table, then falls back perfectly in place.

The next song on the tape is "It's Raining Men." Pearl is imitating John's long-legged way of dancing, to the delight of everyone around her—even Suzanne, who now stands on the periphery of the patio, clapping her hands and throwing her head back in full laughter. Now she stumbles over to the table where Herb is sitting with Miriam and Lynnette and reaches out her hands. "Let's dance," she says. "Come on, Herb, come dance with your wife. For old time's sake."

Herb looks up at her, confused. "Go ahead, Herb," Miriam says. "I think it's a lovely idea." She smiles. As for Lynnette—Lynnette's eyes bulge. Her make-up has smeared in purple and black circles under her eyes; sitting there, she looks like an old cartoon illustration of Satan Suzanne saw once, arrived uninvited at some absurdly genteel dinner party. He sat at the table in all his hideousness, and no one in the picture seemed to notice. The caption read: "The Unexpected Guest."

"Suzanne, please," Herb says. "I really don't want to dance."

"But it's all right with Miriam, isn't it?" says Suzanne.

"Go ahead, don't stop on my account," Miriam says.

Suzanne grabs Herb's hands and hoists him up. "Come on," she says loudly, so that several of her relatives turn and look. "We'll show these young people what dancing really is."

Herb has no choice but to go with her. She drags him between two of her cousins into the center of the patio, where John and Pearl are still going strong.

Pearl, who has been enjoying her spotlight, gives her daughter a look of irritation and suspicion. "Come on, Mom," Suzanne says. "You can't hog all the attention all night." And she grabs Herb's hands, and swings him into a jitterbug.

But "It's Raining Men" ends. The next song on the tape, inexplicably, is "Smoke Gets in Your Eyes." John gets down on his knees and begs Pearl, who shoos him off. "No, I just can't anymore," she says. "I'm just too tired."

"Oh, you'll break my heart," John says. "My heart is breaking."

"Good to see you haven't forgotten how to flirt, Mama," Suzanne says to Pearl, and everyone laughs. She has grabbed Herb firmly around the waist, to make sure he doesn't try to run away from the slow dance. Now, alone in the circle, they writhe, Herb trying to keep his distance, Suzanne insistently holding him down so that his chest pushes against hers.

"Hey," Herb says, "I have an idea. Let's make this a family dance. Let's have the whole family. Come on, Seth!"

Everyone roars approval. Seth nods no, but it's only for show. His grandmother pushes him out into the opening arms of his parents, who take him in. The song continues, and the three of them roll haphazardly over the patio. "When an old flame dies," Suzanne sings, "you know what happens."

There is a sound of rustling, now, behind the circle. Someone is trying to persuade Lynnette to join the dance. Indeed, several of her aunts have hoisted her up, and are pushing her toward the makeshift dance floor, refusing to heed her insistent pleas that she does not want to dance.

"Come on," Pearl says. "Don't be a spoilsport. Dance with the family, darling."

But a spoilsport is exactly what Lynnette wants to be. "I don't want to," she says through gritted teeth, and elbows her way out of her aunts' grips. To no avail. A space has cleared in the circle, and John has grabbed Lynnette by the arm so firmly that tears spring to her eyes. "Come on," he says. "Dance."

"Let me go or I'll scream," Lynnette warns him.

"Shut up and don't be a baby," John says, and plummets her into the center of the circle, into the reeling inner circle of her family.

Immediately they close around her, like a mouth. It is dank inside that circle, full of the smells of alcohol and perfume. Arms around arms, heads knocking, the family stumbles, barely able to keep its balance. "I love you, sweetie," Suzanne says from somewhere, and a mouth nuzzles Lynnette's hair.

She is crying now. Besides the music, her crying is the only sound, for the crowd has suddenly been struck silent, and is watching with wide eyes. And though Herb's hand squeezes her shoulder, though he whispers in her ear, "It's all right, honey," all she feels is the terror of inertia, like the last time he ever pushed her on the swing. Higher and higher she went, as if his strength could disprove her fatness. "Daddy, stop!" she had screamed as the swing rose. "Stop, stop, I'm scared!" Her hands clutched the metal chains, her mouth opened. She wasn't scared of the height; she was scared of him, of how he kept pushing, as if the swing were magic, and by pushing he could change her forever into the pretty little girl he really wanted to be his partner.

Radiation

T wo sisters and a brother were sitting at a kitchen table watching "General Hospital."

Is Monica good now, or bad, asked the younger sister, a girl of eight.

I can't tell, said the brother, who had just returned from a summer program for college-bound youths.

Shut up, shut up, I can't hear, said the oldest sister, waving away a fly attracted to her damp skin.

First she was bad, I think, then she was good, but now she's bad again, said the cleaning lady, who had been intimate with the show since its inception.

The younger sister got up and ran across the house to her mother's room. On the way, she played a game of her own invention involving somersaults and spinning.

The mother was riding the Exercycle, and also watching "General Hospital."

Again the girl asked, Is Monica good or bad?

I don't know, said the mother, pushing up and back against the handlebars to improve muscle tone. I can never tell.

On the screen Monica and Lesley were arguing over Rick.

An alarm went off, a commercial came on. The mother stepped off the Exercycle, sat down at the make-up vanity, and began combing her hair. She had it cut specially by a hairdresser who specialized in ladies undergoing the treatment. As the comb went through, lifting each tuft from the scalp, it revealed the concealed bald patches.

Want to go with me to the radiation therapy center? the mother asked the daughter.

Nah, I'd rather watch, the daughter said. Bear and Ivy'll go, though. They've never been yet.

No, the mother said, they haven't. She put on her lipstick, then dabbed off the excess with a Kleenex.

Kids, you ready to go? the mother asked, walking into the kitchen.

We are, said the older daughter.

Just remember to put on your shoes, will you? the mother said.

The older sister looked at her brother and grimaced, sucking in her cheeks and curling her tongue in a way that six out of every seven people can do. Then she touched the tip of her nose with the tip of her tongue, smiled, and said in falsetto, Yes, Mother dear.

In the car, the son, who was called Bear, lay down along the full length of the back seat. His sister, who was undergoing psychotherapy as part of her training to be a psychotherapist, was explaining that often children who have had abnormally close relationships with their parents are unable to break away from them when they become adults. Consequently, they deal with their aggression by "rebelling" over and over again, well into adulthood, rather than simply letting go, saying, my parents are this way, and I accept them this way. And that, she went on to explain, was why her old best friend Katie had done what she had done.

What she had done was go through the motions of a full wedding to her boyfriend when in actuality they had never even gotten a marriage license.

In addition, the ceremony had been questionable, what with each vowing to love, honor, cherish, and always be ready to fuck the other.

So you see, the daughter finished, it's a very complicated situation when viewed psychologically.

The mother didn't see it that way. Her main point was, what a rotten kid, what a rotten thing to do. Keith, Katie's father, her *father*, she reasoned, is dying and he wants to see his daughter married before he goes. Is that too much? Is it? I always knew Katie was a sneak, the mother said. Out for herself. Selfish.

The daughter twisted in the seat and again stuck her tongue out. It's more complicated, she said again. I don't see anything complicated about it, the mother said.

Look, the daughter said. You know what I mean.

While she talked she played with the electric window.

Look, she said, Corinne's in a weird way—

Don't play with the electric window, it's already been broken once this year.

Corinne, the daughter began again, is in a weird way jealous of Keith.

Corinne was Keith's wife, getting a Ph.D. late in life.

Jealous! the mother said. Jealous of a dying man. She can't wait until—

Look! Now the daughter began to play with the seatbelt. She almost wishes it was her dying because she thinks she's so much more unhappy than he is, and she wants to justify her suffering. I think she's actually glad Katie and Evan didn't get married, even though she wouldn't admit it.

I don't buy it, the mother said. Corinne's a sneak, too. Jealous! If she was jealous, why would she want to marry your father?

What?

The son, lying in back, sat up.

What? he said again.

It's nothing, Bear, said the daughter.

Come on, Ivy, he's old enough now, the mother said. All it is, Bear, is that once Corinne got drunk and told Daddy that when I died and Keith died they could get married.

The son laughed nervously, perhaps relievedly. You're kidding, he said.

And don't you dare mention this to anyone, the mother said, especially your little sister.

Of course I won't, the son said, of course not.

By this time they had reached the radiation therapy center, which was new and modern and underground. They took an elevator down and emerged in a large, plush waiting room with carpeted walls.

Wow, the sister said.

Isn't this nice? the mother said, smiling. She led them through. It was nice. All the tables had backgammon boards and chess boards built into them. There were Folons and O'Keeffes and Wyeths on the walls. There were books and magazines, toys and puzzles for kids. The colors were bright and cheerful, but not so bright and cheerful as to leer at the dying, the architect having conferred with a noted death-and-dying specialist on the design.

Isn't this nice, Bear? the mother said. See through the glass? That's where they do the treatment.

Behind a big glass pane—too big to be called a window—the son could see a flat, silver table that looked cold. It stood like an island in the center of a room behind the glass. Above it, a large machine, resembling a machine gun, pointed down from the ceiling.

They walked over to the nurses' station.

Hello, Joanne, the mother said to the nurse.

Good to see you again, Gretl, the nurse said. These your kids?

They sure are, the mother said. This is Ivy, and this is George, but we call him Bear.

Your mom talks a lot about you, honey, the nurse said to the son. How's the new lawn furniture? You get it yet?

We sure did, the mother said. It's great. But you know, furniture you leave outside, it always gets ruined. I don't count on it lasting more than a year.

Well, said the nurse, Frank and I have had the same set for almost three years now. Where'd you get yours?

The son turned from the conversation to watch an older man emerge from the row of dressing cubicles. His sister watched him watch. The older man had put on a white robe which tied around the back. He still had on his black business shoes and short black socks; his legs were skinny and white. Having taken a moment to light his pipe, he sat down in a corner and read a copy of *Time*.

Nearby a couple of little girls played Chutes and Ladders. He remembered his little sister told him, there were always kids to play with at the radiation therapy center.

Lurene was asking for you, the nurse said. Too bad you missed her.

Lurene was a character the son had heard of, part of his mother's dinnertime monologue of her life at the radiation therapy center. She was old, a phone operator, and she had the same disease the mother had, only in the earlier stages. She was frightened because the doctors gave her contradictory reports. But the mother prevailed, took her under her wing, told her what was what, offered her whole living self as evidence that it could be got through.

Now Lurene knew what was what.

The mother had gone into a little cubicle to change, so the brother and sister sat down. The brother picked up a copy of *Highlights*; the sister chewed her hair.

Bear up, Bear, the sister said.

The son put down the magazine.

It's just I don't like this place. She pretends it's so happy, why pretend she likes to come here?

People cope in different ways, the sister said, trying not to sound holier-than-thou.

I don't know, the brother said. I guess I'll feel better when Daddy gets home. Things are better when he's here.

He turned back to the magazine. He started to read the "Goofus and Gallant" column.

Bear, the sister asked, are you still upset about what Corinne said?

Yes. No. I guess I am, the brother said. I don't know. I just think, she put him through college. Three hundred sixty-five days a year, welding battleships to put him through college. It'd be nice if he didn't have to travel so much.

He returned to the magazine.

You know they have problems, Bear, the sister said, big problems. There's so much anger between them. But anger's different than hate, Bear.

It's not like she's going to die in a year, the brother said from inside the magazine. Corinne wants to make Mama sicker than she is.

Bear . . .

Don't say it, Ivy, the brother said, standing up. You think you know so much. I've lived with them. He does love her. More than you know. Maybe even more than he knows. I tell you, I've seen it. There are things none of us know, things you don't—

Bear, when are you going to face the fact—

But he had turned from her.

The mother came out again, in a white hospital gown, smiling big.

Isn't this the height of fashion, she joked, turning a pirouette. The son laughed. Through the slightly parted back of the gown, he could see small legs, her bra, her large flowered underpants—briefs, they called them in ladies' stores, as opposed to panties.

She went behind the glass and lay down on the table. The son stood to watch. He thought he saw her flinch as her skin touched the cold metal. He could see on the far side of the glass a technician operating the controls.

Once, twice, the machine went over her in a dark sweep. She had to lie perfectly still. You couldn't see it, the miraculous, burning radiation that was making the lumps go down.

I wonder how it works, the sister said. But her brother wasn't listening. He had his whole face pressed against the glass. He was remembering stories his mother had told him, he thought, to anguish him. About the boy who stole her lunch every day for a year; about the doctor they said was going to just give her a check-up, but forced her down on the dining room table and tore her tonsils out; about the dog she had when she was first married, the dog named Brownie who was poisoned for no good reason by a psychotic neighbor, and that was why they never got a dog as children. And he remembered how a year ago she had told his father, maybe I'll go to Italy with you this year, and the father, in some private hour, told her, no, he did not want her to go to Italy with him and she had said fine, fine, that's just fine, I'll stay here. I have the pool, my friends, everything I need, and when she told her son about it she warned him, don't you dare tell your father I told you, I still have some pride.

No, the son thought, he would remember the other stories. Stories she told when she was drunk or happy. Stories of the docks where she welded. I was the best in my division, she had told him. But I was a woman, so I never got a raise. If it were today, I would've complained.

Then she modelled lady welder uniforms. The unions were crooked. Italian men traded her hot eggplant sandwiches made by their wives in the ghetto for her tuna on toast. And the son knew they wanted her in her tight metal suit.

All that was long ago, she would finish.

Why don't you weld again?

I couldn't ever. I'm too old, Bear, too set in my ways.

He looked at her through the glass. The machine passed over her again. He wanted very much to touch her through the glass. But of course he could not.

She still lay perfectly still. He heard his sister gasp. He turned, and she was bent over, her hand on her mouth, her eyes red, choking back a fit of tears that had come over her like a cough. Then the normal light went on. The mother got up. She came out.

Is that all? the son asked.

That's it, that's all. Simple as one-two-three.

I have to go to the bathroom, the sister said, running.

Eventually she came out. The mother got dressed. They left.

When they got home, the younger sister and the cleaning lady were watching "The Edge of Night." The younger sister had been indulged, and had baked cookies, so the kitchen was filled with bowls and knives and pans, all sticky with grease and dried dough.

April doesn't know Draper's alive, and she's gonna marry Logan, the younger sister said excitedly. And they're gonna kidnap Emily to get Kirk's money, but Kirk's not Kirk, he's Draper.

Oh, my God, the mother said, staring at the filthy kitchen. Goddammit, I told you never to do this unless you asked me first. You cook, and I have to clean up all your goddamned messes. It's not fair. It's just not fair.

She lifted her hands toward them all, whether to push them away or embrace them none could tell. She looked at them, and her face twisted like when she had the palsy. Then she turned from them. They could hear her sobbing as she ran down the hallway.

Her children were stunned. Though they were used to her annoyance with them, they were not used to crying. They sat there. The younger daughter began to hum.

It's funny how people on soap operas die on one show and come back on another, the girl said.

So on earth, in heaven, answered the cleaning lady.

The other two were silent. The son stood and walked to his mother's room, ignoring the sister's warnings.

Her bedroom door was closed. He stood outside it for what seemed a long time. Finally he knocked. She didn't answer. He opened the door gently. On her huge bed the mother lay curled, very small, weeping quietly. He stood back from her.

Ma, he said.

She didn't answer. The crying had stopped, replaced by heaves.

Ma, he said again.

She did not look up. It's O.K., Bear, I'm all right, she managed to say.

The son wanted to hug her then, but he knew he couldn't. Something held him back—what had always held him back. There were rules.

I hope you'll feel better, Mama, he said. Then he left the room.

She nodded. She was glad he was gone. It annoyed her to have to comfort him in her suffering.

Once I knew a sailor, she sang to herself, a sailor from the sea . . . and she thought of her own mother, with too many children and no English.

Gradually she got up. She dried her eyes, blew her nose. Standing in front of the mirror, she pulled violently at the short hairs. None came out. Well, she thought, another day. Still, perhaps she would take her hairdresser's advice and get a wig. Funny how with time one can grow accustomed to even the most frightening changes; how even the unimaginable can become manageable.

There, she would be fine. She would apologize and dinner would be fine. Why, just five years ago, the tests she now sat through routinely, without flinching, would have made her faint with pain. She would have vomited at the sight of the scars on her body. She would have wept for fear of death. No more.

But looking at herself in the mirror, she remembered the rebellious girl she had once been, and she was only sorry she could not find it in herself to be courageous.

Out Here

They line up, from eldest to youngest: Gretchen, Carola, Jill. Leonard frames them in his viewfinder. When they stand together, posed, he can see similarities—the arcs of cheekbones, almond-shaped eyes, thin lips—but if these women were strangers to him and he met them separately, he would never guess that they were sisters. Gretchen, Leonard's wife, is the tallest as well as the oldest. As she arranges herself, she shakes out her hair and laughs. Carola—hair shorter, mouth smaller than her sisters'—sighs loudly. Jill, standing barefoot next to her, jumps from one foot to the other on the hot cement.

"Hurry up, Leonard. I have to get dinner," Carola says.

"Just let me focus," Leonard says.

The sisters grumble and link arms. Through his camera, Leonard thinks, he has captured an image that has nothing to do with these women as individuals but, rather, with how they lean away from one another, how their arms strain against touching.

"It's too hot to stand like this much longer," Jill says. She unlinks her arm from Carola's to brush away a fly.

He takes the picture. The camera spews out a piece of photo-
graphic paper, fog green. Immediately the sisters disentangle and go
back to what they were doing—Gretchen to the porch, Carola to the
kitchen, Jill hopping from stone to stone across the lawn to where
her friend Donna Lee sits leaning against a maple tree, reading.
Leonard shades the picture with his left hand and, squinting, bends
over to watch the image emerge.

Even though they both live in New York City, Carola and Jill hardly
ever see each other, and never on social occasions. They have been
meeting only to haggle about bank accounts, trust funds, their
father's health-insurance policy. Carola works at a publishing
company, in subsidiary rights, and lives on the East Side; Jill lives
with Donna Lee in a nameless region just below Tribeca, and is doing
temp work to pay for a film course at NYU. Gretchen has been living
in Mill Valley, in Northern California, since college, and for the past
three years she has been married to Leonard, who has a job with a
software company. What has brought the sisters together again now
is the death of their father. He died of emphysema, in his late sixties,
and they have gathered in an old house in Connecticut that is not
"the old house" but a house completely unfamiliar to them. Their
father moved into it three years ago, after their mother's death and
his almost immediate remarriage to a divorcée named Eleanor
Manley. It is Eleanor's "old house." She died six months ago of a
stroke; her children then cleaned the house of its knickknacks,
scrubbed it as best they could of early memories, and left it to the
widower, whom none of them knew very well. In spite of this recent
cleaning, there are still hints of another family's life here that has
nothing to do with Gretchen, Carola, or Jill. They have come to sort
through the few things their father brought with him when he moved
here.

Jill has never been to the house before. Gretchen and Carola visited once, two years ago, in the summer. Jill refused to come that time, without explanation. It is a nineteenth-century stone house, with turrets, and ivy climbing up the walls. "Stately," the Westport real estate agents would say. That summer, Eleanor's mark was everywhere: The beds were made with flowered sheets, the halls lined with her photographs of Parisian street urchins. There were saltcellars and little pepper mills at each place at dinner, chairs with paws. The house, Carola thought, was so quintessentially Eleanor's domain that she doubted whether her father could have felt very comfortable there. Even Eleanor's children seemed to have no interest, no stake in it. Of course, Eleanor is gone now, and their father is gone. Still, his children walk the halls quietly, like invaders.

"Leonard and I are going to think of this as a vacation," Gretchen said at dinner the first night they arrived, four days ago. "A healthful retreat." They would get up at six, she said, and run—five, six miles— and in the afternoon they would do exercises. She would work out a regimen for each of them. And they should eat as little sugar and salt as possible, Gretchen told Carola, who had put herself in charge of cooking. Gretchen ate hardly any salt, and was in marvellous shape— her skin bronzed, her hair golden, her body lean.

"You're not getting me up at six," Carola said, sticking out her tongue and with great deliberateness salting her meat.

"I'll run," Jill said. "And Donna Lee will run. Donna Lee used to be a track star."

Donna Lee, surprised to be mentioned, paused in the midst of putting a forkful of stuffing into her mouth, blushed, and smiled. Everyone looked at the table.

"Tomorrow morning, then," Gretchen said. "Carola can decide if she wants to join us."

*   *   *

Now, in the late-afternoon sunlight, Jill, her face smudged, is climbing a tree. There are twigs in her clothes and in her hair, which hangs down to her waist. Donna Lee is watching her from behind her book, while on the porch Gretchen is watching Donna Lee. The porch is far enough away so that Gretchen can say to Leonard, "What *is* the story with that girl?"

He shakes his head, and gazes absently at the line of maples bordering the lawn. He is disappointed because no one cares about his photograph. He showed it to Gretchen, and she brushed it off—glanced at it, said, "Neat," and put it down next to her iced coffee.

"I'm still puzzled," Gretchen says. "She's nice enough, I suppose, but she's so withdrawn. It's impossible to talk to her. She's on her guard every second."

"She's probably scared."

"Why?"

"Coming into a strange family is scary," Leonard says. "You feel like an intruder. Especially at a time like this."

Gretchen puts on her sunglasses and lies back in the chair. "Jill probably shouldn't have brought her," she says.

"Young love," Leonard murmurs.

"*What?*"

He turns, and Gretchen is staring straight at him.

Carola, in the kitchen, notices through the window how suddenly Gretchen has turned her head, and is pleased to see her taken off her guard, particularly by Leonard. The kitchen is hot. Carola has cooked every meal so far; she feels in control, at ease, only in the kitchen. This is why she refuses when Donna Lee and Gretchen offer to help. She knows they're only doing it to be polite, and she'd rather not have their help anyway. It has been her experience that people who try to help in the kitchen usually end up just milling around—getting in the way and nibbling at the food. Carola hates to have anyone touch the food before it's served. Her father used to infuriate her by eating spoonfuls of jam right from the jar. He and Gretchen and Jill always came into the kitchen and disrupted everything just when dinner was ready. Gretchen picked the bacon out of the salad, Jill refused to eat what their mother had prepared and made herself a grilled-cheese sandwich. And then they all disappeared when the dishes had to be done—all but Carola. She would stay and help her mother dry.

Outside the window, Gretchen and Leonard appear to have stopped talking for the moment. Jill has climbed down from the tree and is leaping about the yard, head back, flinging out her hair like a mane.

"She is a child," Carola says out loud, mostly to hear how it sounds, and breaks an egg into a bowl. As for Gretchen, she is simply selfish. Both of them all but abandoned the family these last years—especially when their mother got sick. Carola alone stuck around, stuck it out, sat day after day by the hospital bed when the cancer started to spread. She knows they resent her, out of guilt, but she also knows she did the right thing, no matter what Gretchen might say.

Tonight, as usual, they will wolf down the dinner she has made them and thank her for it only in the most cursory way, if at all. Especially Donna Lee. Carola does not like that woman. Last night, when everyone else had carefully counted out the shrimp, to make sure that each person got the same amount, Donna Lee simply reached the spoon onto the platter and took a huge heap—at least twice as much as anyone else. And then halfway through the meal, embarrassed, she tried to shovel them back onto the platter when no one was looking.

Leonard is rapping at the window, waving. Carola smiles at him. Her scalp itches from the steam, making her long to wash her hair.

But she washes her hair too often, she has decided; it's getting brittle. She takes all of her hair in her left hand and pulls until it hurts, then lets it spring back.

Leonard walks into the kitchen. "What is she doing?" he asks Carola. He points out the window at Jill, who is galloping back and forth across the lawn, making wheezing noises.

"She's pretending to be a horse," Carola says.

Leonard looks at her, confused more by her nonchalance than by Jill's strange cavorting.

"She's done it forever," Carola says. "Since we were kids. She calls it playing horse."

"I see," Leonard says. "Are there rules to the game?"

"Oh, in Jill's mind there's probably a very complicated set of rules."

Leonard smiles, and returns to gazing out the window at Jill. In this strange house, Leonard is awed by the women who surround him—women who paint their fingernails, wear tiger-striped underwear, were once track stars. Women who run in circles pretending that they are horses.

Leonard has never before been to the East Coast. The world of the East is different, he has decided. Because his own family is so close-knit, he is puzzled by Gretchen's sisters, and wonders how they could have splintered and lost touch so easily. And he is puzzled by the landscape. He can cope with desert, and wild plains of brush, and yellow hills, but these green, green lawns and trees make him feel as if he were in some foreign land.

"Can I see your photograph?" Carola asks, and Leonard turns, suddenly shaken out of his reverie, to see that she is staring at him.

"Sure," he says, and fishes in his back pocket. "Here it is."

He hands her the snapshot, and immediately her face seems to break. "Oh, I look horrible," she says.

"No, you don't," Leonard says, as he takes the picture back from her. "You look great. But something's missing. When I took this picture, I saw something that didn't have to do with any one of you. It had to do with all of you, really. I'm not good at explaining things. Whatever it was, it's not in the picture."

"It's not something that's missing," Carola says. "It's what's there. It's me. I'm ugly in pictures. Also, my hair's dirty; is there time for me to wash it before dinner?"

"Look at her," Leonard says, and gazes at Jill, who is still galloping across the yard.

Jill is still running back and forth, neighing, her hair flying, when Leonard goes back out to the porch. "Perhaps she really thinks she is a horse," he says to Gretchen, but she isn't listening. Across the lawn, Donna Lee leans against the maple tree, reading, or pretend-ing to read. In fact she is absorbed by the gargantuan image of her own eyeball, staring back at her, reflected in the left lens of her glasses. They always stare at her, Jill's sisters. They scrutinize her, their faces full of curiosity and disapproval. The other day, Gretchen asked her what her parents did. "My mother's a librarian," Donna Lee said. "Oh, I see," Gretchen said, and then—nothing. The long, horrible pause that comes when it is too early for a conversation to end, too late to keep it from starting.

Donna Lee puts down her book and stands up, arching her back against the tree. Jill stops in the midst of a gallop and, laughing, falls against Donna Lee, her breath coming hard. Donna Lee can see Gretchen and Leonard on the porch trying not to stare. She still wakes up each morning convinced that Jill will have tired of her, be gone. The winter they met, Jill wore a green down jacket that she kept buttoned down to her knees, and Donna Lee used to tease her, tell-ing her she looked like a giant Chiclet. She loves Jill.

"I'm tired," Jill says, pulling Donna Lee down to the ground with her. "I haven't done that in ages. When I was a kid I could play horse for hours. I used to like to spin, too. I'd just twirl, like a top. Everyone thought I was nuts. But I liked the way everything blurred and only my own body stayed in focus."

Carola, in an upstairs window, looks down at them. She is standing in her father's bedroom, the room he died in. It is a woman's room, with a pink satin comforter on the bed, a huge armoire in the corner, a mirror surrounded by light bulbs. Since she began to clean the room out, Carola has found medicines, a pile of spy novels, rubbing alcohol, and brandy. She had hoped to find some pornographic magazines, some sign of impropriety and decay. She had hoped to find something she could hold against him.

Even now, two weeks after his death, the room smells of her father's cigars and after-shave. It was different when her mother was dying. Her mother left no smell. She packed up everything before she went to the hospital, and when she died she was gone without a trace. Carola never saw the body—just a stripped mattress where an hour before her mother had lain, pale and thin, and asked for a copy of *Vogue*. Carola had been living at home for three months, and visited the hospital every day. Yet when her mother died, it was not in her arms, or even in her presence. She died alone, while Carola was out of the room. When she came back, *Vogue* in hand, there was the stripped mattress, the half-empty water glass. Her mother had died while Carola was sitting in the cafeteria, drinking her coffee and thumbing through *Cosmopolitan*. It had not seemed fair to Carola, and she wanted to call out to her mother to come back, if only to say a proper goodbye. She wanted to rage against this abandonment. After her mother's death, there was no home to be responsible to anymore, and her father put the house on the market. She moved to

New York, found an apartment and a job, but the life she has been leading does not seem real to her, and with perverse nostalgia she thinks back on the year of her mother's dying as the happiest of her life.

Carola does not like to remember these things. She moves to her father's bureau. Every day, she has forced herself to open one drawer and sort through its contents. Today it is the bottom drawer, which contains things of Eleanor's—some silk scarves, old photographs, jewels, and perfume bottles. Perhaps they are things her father could not bear to part with when Eleanor died. They remind Carola that her father loved Eleanor—perhaps more than he loved her mother, and while he was still married.

Eleanor and Carola met only once before her father's second marriage. That was when she was seventeen, and travelling in Europe; her father arranged for her to stay with Eleanor in Paris, where she was living for the year. Eleanor was divorced by then. She courted Carola that week—took her out to dinner, and to Montmartre late at night. Every time they ate, Carola tried to pay for her share, but Eleanor wouldn't allow it. Before Carola left, Eleanor bought her an expensive orange silk scarf with streaks of brilliant blue. Back then, when she knew nothing, Carola idolized Eleanor. It was only years later that she was able to put the visit into a larger perspective.

There is no need to save these things. The photographs are of no one Carola knows, and the scarves are garish; besides, whatever meaning they once had is buried with her father. She has a hard enough time with her own nostalgia; she does not have room for his as well. But, Carola decides, she will keep the jewelry and the perfume bottles. Someone might want them, or they can be sold at a garage sale.

*   *   *

While Carola is going through the drawer, Gretchen and Leonard move upstairs to their room and make love. In the next room, Jill and Donna Lee are resting. Donna Lee's arms are wrapped around Jill's waist, her face buried in Jill's stomach. She is snoring, and Jill—her eyes closed—is weaving her fingers through Donna Lee's hair.

They all sit down to dinner at eight o'clock. Gretchen is examining one of the perfume bottles Carola found, which Gretchen likes and has decided to keep. Leonard is telling everyone about some young men who hatched a plot to turn Marin County into a medieval fiefdom by setting up a laser gun on top of Mt. Tamalpais. They planned a strategic reorganization of society, re-creating a world of serfs and vassals, round tables and court ladies. When a friend got wind of the plot, the young men murdered him in his garage, and were exposed. It was all baffling, insane, yet Leonard sometimes longingly imagines what castles would look like perched on the rough, dry hills, shrouded in fog.

"What I think is so funny," Gretchen says, "is the idea of Marin County as a fiefdom. Can you imagine? I mean, you can't tell the lord he's invading your personal space when he comes around to make you his serf." She laughs, and Carola stares at her. All through her girlhood, Gretchen had boyfriends; she would never give up one until she had found another. She had that kind of control.

Carola is not eating the meal she spent most of the afternoon preparing. Instead, she has brought in from the kitchen a Styrofoam cup of tea and a bowl of tomato soup, which she now stabs at with her fork. (She has forgotten to put out spoons.) She has poured most of her tea out of the cup and into her water glass and shredded the top half of the cup, making a little pile of Styrofoam pieces on her plate.

"Everyone thinks California is so weird," Leonard is saying, rather defensively. "If you ask me, it's the other way around. People are pretty strange out here. No one's polite, everyone pushes and shoves. I think California's fairly civilized, by and large."

No one says anything to this. Carola has captured everyone's attention by making a boat from her Styrofoam cup and floating it in the soup. Now she is pushing the cup back and forth. The red soup crawls slowly up the sides.

"I have a question for everyone," Carola says. "What if you got stuck on a desert island and you only had one piece of paper and one pen? What would you do?"

Sitting across the table, Gretchen puts her hand to her forehead and wonders how Carola has survived alone for so long. And now—right here, of all places—is she going to have a breakdown? She looks at Leonard, who will be no help to her; he never is in crises. And Jill will run away, as she always does.

The Styrofoam cup has finally sunk. Carola is pathetic, Gretchen thinks. Sad. She could be pretty. Who but Carola would worry about being stuck on a desert island? If she would only take herself in hand and *do* something, half the problem would be solved right there. Gretchen wishes that she could sympathize with Carola, but instead she wants to take her by the shoulders and shake some sense into her.

"I think," Donna Lee says, "that I would only allow myself to write one sentence a week, and that in a very small hand. It would probably be a quite marvellous sentence, given that I'd have a week to think about it before writing it down." It is the first thing she has said at dinner all week that was not required of her.

Carola looks at Donna Lee and smiles. "It's good to know that I'm not the only person in the world who thinks about this kind of thing. Thank you."

Jill drops her fork and falls into a sudden convulsion of laughter. Carola, looking at her, begins to laugh, too, and then Leonard and

Gretchen, not because they understand what Jill is laughing at but because the laughter itself is contagious. Only Donna Lee doesn't laugh. There is nothing left on her plate; adrift, she stares at Jill helplessly for direction.

"I'm sorry," Jill says. "I was just remembering that time when Mom was in a bad mood and Daddy put on one of her scarves and did a little imitation of her. He came up behind her and kind of growled and shook his hands. Even she started laughing, he looked so funny. I laugh every time I think of how he looked that day."

As soon as Jill starts to tell the story, everyone stops laughing. Another instance of her father's cruelty, Carola is thinking—to mimic her mother's sorrow, to make it so funny even she had to laugh. How could her mother have loved him so much? He had a lover and he made fun of his wife, yet she was devoted to him. In sickness, she insisted that he be with her, calling out for him in her sleep. He was always there, those last days. Toward the end, belief in responsibility was the only thing that he and Carola shared.

The subject has switched now. Leonard is back on California, its joys and civilities. He's a little drunk, and he waves his fist as he speaks. "Where I grew up," he says, "family meant something. Connections meant something. My brothers and sisters and I always go home for Christmas, every year, and I call my mother every week. But your family! It's terrible how split up you are, all of you so isolated from your father. There's no shared ground, no homestead. It's been lost."

"It never existed," Carola says. "It never was in the first place."

"Oh, that's not true," Gretchen says. "There was lots of family feeling when we were growing up. You've just made yourself forget it."

"And you've made yourself forget all the nights of no one saying a word at dinner," Carola says. "Of Mom and Dad fighting. You and Jill couldn't wait to get away on your own."

"No institution," Jill says, "has been more destructive to women than the nuclear family."

They all look at her, rather puzzled by this generalization.

"What!" Leonard yells. "I'll tell you, I have six sisters, and growing up the way they did they're all better for it."

Jill smiles and shakes her head. "You miss my point," she says. "It's a means of exploitation. Since the sixteenth century, the nuclear family has fit in perfectly with the capitalist system and its whole exploitative program of gender roles. And nothing has caused more psychological damage to women. Fortunately, it's breaking up now."

"How breaking up? What do you mean?" Gretchen asks.

"I mean the divorce rate, the alternatives that women are finding."

Donna Lee looks at the table. Carola grips the edges of her chair. Her eyes are getting wide. "You're one to talk," she says, nearly inaudibly.

"What?"

"I said you're one to talk," Carola says again, slightly more loudly. She looks around, alarmed at having suddenly changed the tenor of the conversation. "I'm sorry," she says. "I just don't see where *you* come off attacking the family."

"Carola, please," Gretchen says, reaching across the table, touching her arm. "Do we have to talk about this now?"

"Oh, let's talk about it," Jill says. "Let's talk about it."

Carola pushes her chair back and sits straight up. "Look," she says. "I don't mean to be confrontational. All I know is it's easy for you to sit there and talk about the demise of the nuclear family and its being a bad thing. You never gave it a chance. You ran away as soon as you could. It's in sickness that families matter, in sickness that they have to pull together, and I just want to ask where were the two of you when Mother got sick?"

"Oh, let's not open this up again," Gretchen says.

"You have no right to say that, Gretchen," Carola says. "I just think there is such a thing as family responsibility. I stuck it out with Mother, you didn't."

"It was your choice," Jill says.

"My responsibility."

"Your choice."

"You can't say I didn't visit," Gretchen says. "I visited three times."

"More than Jill can say," Carola says.

"I made a clean, healthy break and forged my own life," Jill says. "Don't blame me because you didn't."

"You ran away," Carola says.

"I didn't owe Daddy anything."

"When parents take care of you, support you, love you for years, you don't owe them anything? That doesn't work for me, I'm sorry."

"I just think you have to ask yourself something, Carola," Gretchen says. "When Mom got sick, did you stick around because she and Daddy needed you or because you needed them?"

Carola's mouth opens slightly. "Just what do you mean by that?" she asks.

"I don't think they needed you nearly as much as you needed them to need you. I think in some ways they would have been better off if you'd gone and made your own life. I'm sorry to be so blunt, Carola, but you asked for it."

Now Carola stands up, kicks her chair away. "Oh, damn you," she says. "Damn you, damn you. You were hardly even there."

"Don't blame us for leading our own lives," Jill says.

"Don't tell me I didn't have a life," Carola says. "It *was* my life. It had to be. Just because I didn't abandon my mother doesn't mean I wasn't alive."

"No one's saying that, Carola," Jill says.

"I really think we've talked about this long enough," Gretchen says. "I really don't think this is very productive."

"Well, in that case, let's all bow to Her Highness and never say another word," Carola says.

"I didn't start it."

"Yes. Of course. I start everything, don't I?"

Gretchen rubs her eyes. "Why are you doing this, Carola?" she asks wearily.

"Because you're talking about my life. You've made it easy for yourself, but you can't tell me I'm invalid. You just can't."

"No one's saying that, Carola," Jill says. "We're saying that you made a choice. We made choices, too."

"You have to accept our lives if you want us to accept yours," Gretchen says. "You have to respect what we chose."

"Excuse me," Donna Lee says, pushing her chair away and walking out of the room. Jill looks over her shoulder.

Carola sits down again, slumping in her chair. There are tears in her eyes. "That's what you can't understand," she says. "Maybe for you, but for me there never was a choice."

The first time Gretchen visited her mother in the hospital, it was in response to a call from Carola. "She may be dying," Carola said flatly—something of an exaggeration, Gretchen found out later. Her mother lay in bed, her weight dropping, her hair falling. The TV ran all day—cartoons, game shows, Mike Douglas, the news. Gretchen flew out on a Friday from California and found Carola in the room, sitting by the bed, crossing and uncrossing her legs. Her father was out getting something to eat. Earlier, Carola had managed to sneak her mother's dog into her room for a visit, and what Gretchen remembers most vividly is that the room smelled of dog—a much more pleasant smell, she thought, than the antiseptic odor she usually associated with hospital rooms. Their mother asked Carola to go to the hospital gift shop and buy her some magazines and eye make-up. Carola was immediately off, grateful to have a purpose. Then her mother beckoned Gretchen closer to her.

"I don't know what to do," she said. "Carola's driving me crazy. She's here every minute. I have to pretend I'm better, just to keep her from feeling guilty. Things are bad enough. I just want her out of here."

"Have you asked Daddy to talk to her?" Gretchen said.

"Yes, yes. He keeps putting it off. She doesn't realize that this has nothing to do with her. It's between me and your father. It's our business, not hers."

What friends of theirs would say, for years afterward, was that their mother used her sickness to keep a hold on him. Of course, it wasn't that simple. Gretchen is convinced that there was a bond—thin as a wire but incredibly tough—that held her parents together. Perhaps it was this bond that Carola had imposed upon. That night, her father finally had a talk with Carola. She stormed out of the house, red-eyed, screaming, "You're not being fair!" Her father followed her to the door, calling her name. Years earlier, he had demanded their dedication, when the number of business trips he took suddenly doubled and their mother started to cry, spontaneously, whenever she did the dishes. He had said, "I'd like you to stick around the house while I'm away, keep your mother company." Only Carola heeded his request, never went out on dates. And now, suddenly, with that generation gone, she is thrown on her own. Though Gretchen has suffered through depression and worry, real pain is something she has rarely felt. Her lack of empathy disturbs her—a sort of dull ache. She knows it is nothing compared to what Carola must feel.

There was another confrontation, two months to the day after their mother's death. Gretchen's father had called the daughters together, in his office, to inform them of his plans to remarry. They sat in chairs in front of his desk, and he stood stiffly and would not look at them. "I'm planning to be married," he said. "To Eleanor Manley. She's been a dear friend for years, and a great comfort. I know this may be hard for you to accept, but I've made my decision. We'll be married in two weeks."

"Mother died so recently," Gretchen said. "Are you sure this is wise?"

He looked at them. "I feel no need to justify this course of action to you," he said. "It's my decision, not yours."

Gretchen clutched her chair, holding herself together against his attack. Jill began to button her coat. Only Carola's eyes narrowed in anger. "How long have you been involved with her?" she asked.

He cracked his knuckles. "For quite some time," he said. "Before your mother's death, but she never knew."

"She knew," Carola said.

"This is none of your business, Carola," their father said.

Jill went back to New York that afternoon. Gretchen and Carola stayed in his house, avoiding him and each other. The house no longer seemed theirs. When Gretchen woke up the next morning, Carola was already gone.

I'd better go talk to her. Someone has to," Gretchen says now to Leonard. They are sitting in the living room, alone. She gets up; Leonard watches her in silence, unsure of what to say or do.

There is a fragrant smell of shampoo in Carola's room. She is sitting on the bed in her bathrobe, a towel wrapped around her head. Gretchen sits down next to her.

"I've decided to go back to New York before the week's over," Carola says. "I have things to do."

"Fine," Gretchen says. "We can finish up here. It's more of a vacation for us."

"Thanks."

"I wanted to apologize," Gretchen says.

"Of course, you know, you're right," Carola says. "About everything. About Mom and Dad. But I'm still angry. To move away—to move to New York, and find that apartment and that job, and keep them—you can't know how hard it was for me just to sustain my life."

"You're right," Gretchen says. "I can't know. I only wish I could."

When she was a teen-ager, Donna Lee liked to become the confidante of girls with boyfriends, so that after the boyfriends left, as they always did, the girls would cry on her shoulder and she could embrace them. It wasn't until years later that she realized what she was doing—contriving intimacy, setting herself up to be let down. Love is still a contrivance for Donna Lee, a yearning for Jill to trust her, to touch her unexpectedly in sleep. She fully expects Jill to forget her at any moment.

"I want to leave," Donna Lee says to Jill after the scene at dinner. "I feel lost."

"I'll leave with you, then," Jill says.

Donna Lee shakes her head, unable to keep from smiling in gratitude. "You should stay," she says.

"This happens whenever I see them. They badger me about running away until I do it. Besides, I have other priorities. I have you to think of."

"Don't worry about me," Donna Lee says, amazed that she could be someone worth thinking of.

In the morning, Jill and Donna Lee are standing on the front porch, packed and ready to go.

"Before you leave," Leonard says to Jill, "let me just ask you one thing. What does it do for you, that horse game?"

Jill smiles. "Let's call it my alternative to the nuclear-family dynamic."

"I see," Leonard says. He laughs and claps his hands. Gretchen smiles at him as if she were his mother. Soon Jill and Carola will be gone; it will be her job to finish the cleaning out. She can be devastated, or she can go about it with a healthy contempt. For what remains in this house is a history about which she can hardly be nostalgic, and memories she would like to move beyond. Perhaps now she can sort through her father's belongings with that blunt dispassion which is the essence of revenge. Perhaps she, too, can be cruel.

"Have a nice trip," Leonard says. "Come visit us in California." And Carola, leaning against the wall of the house, waves, thinking that if she were on that desert island she would not write a word on the piece of paper. She would invent an alphabet of folding—an impermanent origami language that would mean nothing to anyone but her. It's her secret answer; she's sure none of the others have thought of it.

Dedicated

C elia is treading the lukewarm blue water of Nathan's parents' swimming pool. It is a cloudless Sunday in late June, the sun high and warm. She is watching the shadows which the waves she makes cast on the bottom of the pool—pulses of light and darkness whose existence is frenzied and brief, so different from the calm, lapping waves they reflect. Celia is at the center. The waves radiate out from where she treads, her arms and legs moving as instinctively as those of a baby held up in the air. Near the French doors to the library, Nathan and Andrew, her best friends, are dancing to a song with a strong disco beat and lyrics in German which emanates from a pair of two-foot-high speakers at either end of the library. The speakers remind Celia of the canvas bases her mother uses for her macramé wall hangings, but she knows that in spite of their simplic- ity, or because of it, they are worth thousands of dollars each, and represent a state-of-the-art technology. Nathan has told her this several times in the course of the weekend; he worries that she or Andrew might knock one of the speakers over, or carelessly topple a precious vase, or spill Tab on one of the leather sofas. They are not rich, he tells them jokingly; they do not know about these things. (The expensiveness of his parents' house is, by both necessity and design, easy to overlook, but Celia's eye for what she does not have has already rooted out the precious, notices that there are fresh bowls of roses in every room and that the gray parachute-cloth sofas are actually made of silver silk.)

The song changes. "Oh, I love this," Andrew says. He is an enthusiastic and uncontrolled dancer. He twists and jolts, and lunges forward accidentally, nearly colliding with one of the speakers. "Will you be careful?" Nathan shouts, and Andrew jumps back onto the patio. "Relax," he says. "I'm not going to break anything."

Celia kicks her legs, pulls her neck back, and gracefully somersaults into the water; suddenly the music is gone, Nathan and Andrew are gone, though she can see their distorted reflections above the pool's surface. She breathes out a steady stream of bubbles, pulls herself head over heels, and emerges once again, sputtering water. The music pounds. They are still fighting. "Andrew, if you don't calm down," Nathan says, "I'm going to turn off the music. I swear."

"Go to hell," Andrew says, and Celia takes another dive, this time headfirst, pulling herself deep into the pool's brightness. She can hear nothing but the sound of the pool cleaning itself—a wet buzz. When she reaches the bottom, she turns around and looks up at the sun refracted through the prisms of the water. She is striped by bars of light. She would stay underwater a long time, but soon she's feeling that familiar pressure, that near-bursting sensation in her lungs, and she has to push off the bottom, swim back up toward the membrane of the water's surface. When she breaks through, she gulps air and opens her eyes wide. The music has been turned off, Andrew is gone, and Nathan is sitting on the chaise next to the pool, staring at his knees.

"You were sitting on the bottom of the pool," he says to Celia.

"What happened? Where's Andrew?" she asks, wiping the chlorine off her lips.

"He stormed off," Nathan says. "Nothing unusual."

"Oh," Celia says. She looks at her legs, which move like two eels under the water. "I wish I knew what to tell you," she says.

"There's nothing to tell."

Celia keeps her head bowed. Her legs seem to be rippling out of existence, swimming away with the tiny waves.

Celia has spent every free moment, this weekend, in the water. She lusts after Nathan's tiled swimming pool, and the luminous crystal liquid which inhabits it. In the water, Celia's body becomes sylph-like, a floating essence, light; she can move with ease, even with grace. On land, she lumbers, her body is heavy and ungainly and must be covered with dark swatches of fabric, with loose skirts and saris. Celia is twenty-three years old, and holds the position of assistant sales director at a publishing company which specializes in legal textbooks. Of course, Nathan and Andrew always encourage her to quit her job and apply for a more creative position somewhere, to move downtown and leave behind her tiny apartment and terrible neighborhood. But Andrew is blessed, and Nathan is rich. They don't understand that things like that don't work out so easily for other people.

Here are Andrew and Nathan, as someone who hasn't known them for very long might see them: blond boy and dark boy, WASP and Jew, easy opposites. They work for rival advertising companies, but work seems to be just about the only thing they don't fight about. Nathan has dark, pitted skin, curly hair, a face always shadowed by the beginnings of a beard, while Andrew is fine-boned and fair, with a spindly, intelligent nose, and a body which in another century might have been described as "slight." He likes to say that he belongs in another century, the nineteenth, in the tea-drinking circle of Oscar Wilde; Nathan is invincibly devoted to present-day. They live on opposite poles of Manhattan—Nathan on the Lower East Side, Andrew in an East Ninety-sixth Street tenement on the perilous border of Harlem. From his window, Andrew can see the point where the ground ruptures and the train tracks out of Grand Central emerge into open air. Three blocks down Park Avenue he can see Nathan's parents' apartment building. Sometimes he runs into Nathan's mother at D'Agostino's, and they chat about the price of tomatoes, and Nathan's mother, who knows nothing, tells Andrew that he really must come to dinner sometime. Publicly, they are ex-lovers and enemies; privately (but everyone guesses) current lovers and (occasionally) friends. As for Celia, she floats between them, suspended in the strange liquid of her love for them—a love, she likes to think, that dares not speak its name.

That is what they look like to their friends from work, to the people they eat dinner with and sleep with, to all those acquaintances who find them interesting and likeable, but have other concerns in their lives.

And what, Celia wonders now, floating in the pool, is she doing here this weekend, when she has sworn time and again never to travel alone with them anywhere, not even to a restaurant? She always ends up in the middle of their battleground, the giver of approval, the spoils which they fight over, forget, and abandon. She tells herself she is here because it is over a hundred degrees in Manhattan, because her super has confided that the old woman across the hall from her apartment hasn't opened the door for days, and he's getting worried. She tells herself she is here because Nathan's parents are in Bermuda, the maid is on vacation, there is the swimming pool and the garden with fresh basil growing in it. And it's true, they've had a good time. Friday, sticky with Penn Station grime, they walked along the beach, ran in the tide, let the dry, hot wind blow against their faces. Saturday, they went into East Hampton, and looked at all the pretty people on the beach, and Celia decided it really wasn't all that surprising that those people should be rich and happy, while she was poor and miserable. They ate salad and watched a rerun of "The Love Boat," and then Nathan and Andrew tucked Celia into Nathan's parents' big bed and disappeared together to another part of the house. She closed her eyes and cursed herself for feeling left out, for being alone, for having come out here in the first place. She tried, and failed, to imagine what they looked like making love. She tried to hear them. Now, Sunday morning, they have begun fighting because the fact that they still sleep together is a source of shame to both of them. And why not? Even Celia is ashamed. She is not supposed to know that Nathan and Andrew still sleep together, but Andrew calls her every time it happens. "I don't even like him," he tells Celia, his voice hoarse and strained. "But he has this power over me which he has to keep reasserting for the sake of his own ego. Well, no more. I'm not going to give in to him anymore." But even as he says these words, she can hear his voice grow hesitant with doubt, desire, love.

Celia swims to the pool ladder and hoists herself onto the deck. She has been in the water so long that her hands and feet have wrinkled and whitened. She wraps a towel around herself, suddenly ashamed of how her thighs bounce out of water, lies down on an empty chaise, and picks up a magazine called *Army Slave* from the patio table between her and Nathan. Andrew bought the magazine as a belated birthday present for Nathan, but neither of them has shown much interest in it this weekend. Now Celia thumbs through the pages—a man in green fatigues sitting on a bunk bed, clutching his groin; then a few shots of the man fornicating with another man, in officer's garb. In the last pages, a third figure shows up, dressed in leather chaps, and looks on from the sidelines. "Do you like it?" Nathan asks. "Does it turn you on?"

"I don't understand what's so erotic about army bases and locker rooms," Celia says. "I mean, I suppose I understand that these are very male places. But still, they're very anti-gay places. I mean, do you find this erotic? Did you find locker rooms erotic when you were growing up? And this guy in the leather—"

Nathan thrusts out his hips and purses his lips. "Oh, don't let's talk about whips and leather. Let's talk about Joan Crawford!" He makes little kissing gestures at Celia.

"Be serious," Celia says. "I was wondering because I want to know, to understand, genuinely."

"From a sociological perspective?" Nathan asks, returning to a normal posture.

"You could call it that," Celia says.

"I'll tell you this," Nathan says. "When draft registration was reintroduced, I saw a magazine with a picture on the cover of it of this very big hairy guy in a torn-up army uniform, staring out at you very lewdly. And underneath him it said, 'The Gay Community salutes the return of the military draft.' It was really very funny."

Celia's eyes light up. "Oh, that's great!" she says. "That's reclamation!"

Nathan doesn't respond, so she returns to the magazine. She picks up a pencil from the table and starts to scribble something in the margin when Andrew appears, seemingly from nowhere, before her and Nathan. "I'm mad," he says. "But I'm not going to play your stupid game and just run away and hide out and sulk. I want to face things."

"Andrew," Nathan says, "explain to Celia why that magazine is a turn-on. Note I do not use the word 'erotic.' "

"Oh, Christ, Celia," Andrew says, "I can't talk about that with you."

"I should've figured you'd be prudish about things like this when I found out you slept in pajamas," Celia says.

"Andrew doesn't want to spoil the integrity of his double life," Nathan says. "He doesn't want you to know that though by day he is your average preppie fashion-conscious fag, by night he goes wild—leather, cowboy hats, water sports. You name it, he's into it."

"Speak for yourself," Andrew says. "You're the one with the double life." He glances significantly at the pool.

"This isn't sociology. This isn't objective curiosity," Celia says. "You should know that by now."

They both look at her, puzzled. She closes her eyes. The sun beats down, and Celia imagines that the temperature has risen ten degrees in the last ten minutes. She opens her eyes again. Andrew has sat down on the end of Nathan's chaise and is berating him.

In a single, swift lunge, Celia pulls herself up and hurls herself into the water.

Celia, Nathan, and Andrew have known each other since their freshman year in college, when they were all in the same introductory English class. For most of that year, however, Nathan and Andrew recognized each other only as "Celia's other friend"; they had no relationship themselves. She recalls the slight nausea she experienced the day when she learned Nathan was gay. Up until that point, she had never known a homosexual, and she felt ashamed for having liked him, shyly as she did, so shyly that she phrased her feelings like that: "I like him," she confided to her roommate, who played varsity hockey. Celia felt ashamed as well for not having known better, and she feared her naïve affection might seem like an insult to Nathan, and turn him against her. Nathan was something new to Celia; she idolized him because he had suffered for being different, and because his difference gave him access to whole realms of experience she knew nothing of. Celia had never had many friends in school, had never been terribly popular, and this had always seemed just to her: She was fat and shy, and she was constantly being reprimanded for being fat and shy. She never considered that she might be "different" in the intense, romantic way Nathan was. She was simply alone, and where Nathan's aloneness was something that ennobled him, hers was something to regret.

At first, Nathan accepted Celia's gestures of affection toward him because she would listen—endlessly, it seemed—and talk to him, respond, as well. She was fascinated by the stories that he told her so willingly, stories about mysterious sexual encounters in men's rooms, adolescent fumblings in changing rooms. Her curiosity grew; she read every book and article she could find on the subject of homosexuality, including explicit diaries of nights spent cruising the docks and beaches, the bars and bathhouses of New York and L.A. and Paris. She read all of Oscar Wilde, and most of Hart Crane. She started to speak up more, to interrupt in class, and found in her underused vocal cords her mother's powerful, Bronx-born timbre, capable of instantly bringing crowds to attention. At their college, it was quite common for women in certain majors—women with long hair and purple clothes and a tendency to talk loudly and quickly and a lot—to spend most of their time in the company of gay men. Celia became the prime example of this accepted social role, so much so that some people started referring to her as the "litmus paper test," and joking that one had only to introduce her to a man to determine his sexual preference. It was not a kind nickname, implying that somehow she drove them to it, but Celia bore it stoically, and worse nicknames as well. She joked that she was the forerunner of a new breed of women who emitted a strange pheromone which turned men gay, and would eventually lead to the end of the human race. All the time she believed herself to be better off for the company she kept. What Celia loved in her gay friends was their willingness to commit themselves to endless analytical talking. Over dinner, over coffee, late at night, they talked and talked, about their friends, their families, about books and movies, about "embodying sexual difference," and always being able to recognize people in the closet. This willingness to talk was something no man Celia had ever known seemed to possess, and she valued it fiercely. Indeed, she could go on forever, all night, and invariably it would be Nathan who would finally drag himself off her flabby sofa and say, "Excuse me, Celia, it's four A.M. I've got to get to bed." After he left, she would lie awake for hours, unable to cease in her own mind the conversation which had finally exhausted him.

As their friendship intensified, she wanted still to probe more deeply, to learn more about Nathan. She knew that he (and, later, Andrew) had a whole life which had nothing, could have nothing to do with her—a life she heard about only occasionally, when she was brave enough to ask (the subject embarrassed Nathan). This life took place primarily in bars—mysterious bastions of maleness which she imagined as being filled with yellow light creeping around dark corners, cigarettes with long fingers of ash always about to crumble, and behind every door, more lewdness, more sexuality, until finally, in her imagination, there was a last door, and behind it—here she drew a blank. She did not know. Of course Nathan scoffed at her when she begged him to take her to a bar. "They're boring, Celia, totally banal," he said. "You'd be disappointed the same way I was." They were just out of college, and Nathan was easily bored by most things.

A few weeks later Andrew arrived in the city. The night he got in he and Celia went to the Village for dinner, and as they walked down

Greenwich Avenue she watched his eyes grow wide, and his head turn, as they passed through the cluster of leather-jacketed men sporting together in front of Uncle Charlie's. The next night he asked Celia to accompany him to another bar he was scared to go to alone (he'd never actually been to a gay bar), and she jumped at the opportunity. At the steel doors of the bar, which was located on a downtown side street, the bouncer looked her over and put out his arm to bar their entrance. "Sorry," he said, "no women allowed"—pronouncing each syllable with dental precision, as if she were a child or a foreigner, someone who barely understood English. No women: There was the lure of the unknown, the unknowable. She could catch riffs of disco music from inside, and whiffs of a strange fragrance, like dirty socks, but slightly sweet. Here she was at the threshold of the world of the men she loved, and she was not being allowed in, because that world would fall apart, its whole structure of exclusive fantasy would be disrupted if she walked into it. "No women," the bouncer said again, as if she hadn't heard him. "It's nothing personal, it's just policy."

"When all the men you love can only love each other," Celia would later tell people—a lot of people—"you can't help but begin to wonder if there's something wrong with being a woman. Even if it goes against every principle you hold, you can't help but wonder." That night she stood before those closed steel doors and shut her eyes and wished, the way a small child wishes, that she could be freed from her loose skirts, her make-up and jewels, her interfering breasts and buttocks. If she could only be stripped and pared, made sleek and svelte like Nathan and Andrew, then she might slip between those doors as easily as the men who hurried past her that night, their hands in their pockets; she might be freed of the rank and untrustworthy baggage of femininity. But all she could do was turn away. Andrew remained near the door. "Well," he said. "Well, what?" Celia asked. "Would you mind terribly much if I went in myself, anyway?" he asked. She saw in his eyes that desperate, hounded look she recognized from the times they'd walked together, and passed good-looking men in the streets; that look she realized was probably on her face tonight as well. There was something behind those doors which was stronger than his love for her, much stronger. She didn't say anything, but walked away into the street, vowing never to go downtown again. On the subway, riding home, she watched a bag lady endlessly and meticulously rearrange her few possessions, and she decided that she would become bitter and ironic, and talk about herself in witticisms, and live alone always. "For most young women," she decided she'd say, "falling in love with a gay man was a rite of passage. For me it became a career." Then she would take a puff—no, a drag—from her cigarette (she would of course have taken up smoking). And laugh. And toss it off.

Celia has made Andrew and Nathan eggs, and garnished each plate with a sprig of watercress and a little tuft of alfalfa sprouts. Now, balancing the plates on her arm, she walks toward the library, where they've retreated from the sun for the afternoon. When she enters the library, she sees Andrew leaning against the windowsill, and Nathan lying with his legs slung over the leather sofa, his head resting on the floor.

"Lunch," Celia says.

"Sundays are always horrible," Andrew says. "No matter what. Especially Sundays in summer."

Nathan does a backflip off the sofa, and makes a loud groaning noise. "Such depression!" he says. "What to do, what to do. We could go tea dancing! That's a lovely little Sunday afternoon tradition at the River Club. Thumping disco, live erotic dancers . . ."

"I'm not going back to the city one more minute before I have to," Celia says.

"Yes," Andrew says. "I'm sure Celia would just love it if we went off tea dancing."

Celia looks at him.

"I'm surprised at you, Andrew," Nathan says. "You usually enjoy dancing tremendously. You usually seem to have a really euphoric time dancing."

"Enough, Nathan," Andrew says.

"Yes, watching Andrew dance is like—it's like—how to describe it? I think we see in Andrew's dancing the complete realization of the mind-body dualism."

He stands up, walks around the sofa, and hoists himself over its back, resuming his upside-down position. "The body in abandon," Nathan continues. "Total unself-consciousness. Nothing which has anything to do with thought."

Celia gives Nathan a glance of disapproval. It is unnecessary; Andrew is on the defensive himself today. "I find your hypocrisy laughable," he says. "One minute you're telling me, 'Why don't you just stop analyzing everything to death?' and the next you're accusing me of not thinking. Get your attacks straight, Nathan."

"Ah," Nathan says, lifting up his head and cocking it (as best he can) at Andrew, "but I'm not criticizing your dancing, Andrew! I'm just extrapolating! Can you imagine what it would be like to never, ever think, really? I think it would be wonderful! You'd just sort of trip along, not particularly enjoying yourself but never having a bad time, either! Never feeling anguish or jealousy—too complicated, too tiring. I know people who are really like that. You see, Celia, Andrew thinks I'm dishonest. He thinks I run scared from the full implications of my sexual choice. He would like my friends, the Peters. Lovers, Celia. They're both named Peter, and they live together, but they're completely promiscuous, and if one has an affair, the other isn't bothered. Peter just has to tell Peter all about it and it's as if Peter's had the affair, too. But they're happy. They've fully integrated their gayness into their lives. Isn't that what we're supposed to do, Andrew?"

He hoists himself up, and sits down again on the sofa, this time normally.

"Don't be ridiculous," Andrew says. "People like that aren't even people."

Celia, sitting cross-legged on the floor, has finished her eggs. Now she reaches for Nathan's plate and picks the watercress off it. Nathan has eaten only a few spoonfuls. At restaurants, Celia often finds herself picking food off other people's plates, completely unintentionally, as if she's lost control over her eating.

Nathan, his head right side up, is humming the tune to the Pete Seeger song "Little Boxes." Now he glances up at Celia. "Shall we sing, my dear?" he asks.

"You can," she says. "I don't ever want to sing that song again."

Nathan sings:

> *"Little faggots in the Village,*
> *And they're all made out of ticky-tacky,*
> *Yes, they're all made out of ticky-tacky,*
> *And they all look just the same.*
> *There's a cowboy and a soldier and a UCLA wrest-i-ler,*
> *And they're all made out of ticky-tacky,*
> *And they all look just the same."*

Andrew bursts out laughing. "That's funny," he says. "When did you make that up?"

"*I* made it up," Celia says. "Walking down the street one night." She smiles, rather bitterly, remembering the evening they walked arm in arm, very drunk, past Uncle Charlie's Downtown and sang that song. Nathan suddenly became very self-conscious, very guilty, and pulled away from Celia. He had a sudden horror of being mistaken for half of a heterosexual couple, particularly here, in front of his favorite bar. "Just remember," he had said to Celia. "I'm not your boyfriend."

"Why do I even speak to you?" Celia had answered. It was right after Andrew had abandoned her outside that other bar. That summer Andrew and Nathan, singly and collectively, stood her up at least fourteen times; twice Nathan, who was living at his parents' place, asked to use her apartment to meet people and she let him. She didn't think she was worth more than that. She was fat, and she was a litmus test. The only men she cared about were gay, and she didn't seem to know many women. She was Typhoid Celia. But finally she got angry, one Sunday, when she was at Jones Beach with Andrew. "Answer me this," she said to him, as they settled down on that stretch of the beach which is the nearly exclusive domain of Puerto Rican families. Andrew wasn't even looking at her; he couldn't keep his head from pulling to the left, straining to catch a glimpse of the gay part of the beach, where Celia had refused to sit. "Answer me this," Celia said again, forcing him to look at her. "A nice hypothetical question along the lines of, would you rather be blind or deaf? Why is it that no matter how much you love your friends, the mere possibility of a one-night stand with someone you probably won't ever see again is enough to make you stand them up, lock them out, pretend they don't exist when you pass them in the street? Why do we always so willingly give up a beloved friend for any lover?"

Even now she could see Andrew's head drifting just slightly to the left. Then he looked at her, pointed a finger at her face, and said, "There's a tea leaf lodged between your front teeth."

Celia doesn't realize until she's doing it that she is eating the last of the alfalfa sprouts off Andrew's plate. In horror, she throws them down. She slaps her hand and swears she won't do it again.

"When are your parents getting back?" Andrew asks.

"Not until tonight," Nathan says. "They're due in at seven."

"I spoke to my parents last week. They said they'd look for me in the TV coverage of the Pride March next week. It really touched me, that they'd say that. I didn't even have to mention that there was going to be a Pride March, they already knew."

Silence from Nathan. Celia gathers her hands into fists.

"Are you going to march this year, Nathan?"

Nathan stands up and walks over to the stereo. "No," he says. He puts a recording of Ravel on the turntable.

"That's too bad," Andrew says.

Celia considers screaming, insisting that they stop right here. Andrew knows that Nathan has never marched, will never march, in the annual Gay Pride Parade, ostensibly because he considers such public displays "stupid," but really because he lives in fear of his parents discovering his homosexuality. The last time she visited him here Nathan and his father sat in the library and talked about stocks. All night he was the perfect son, the obedient little boy, but on the train ride back he bit his thumbnail and would not speak. "Do you want to talk about it?" Celia asked him, and he shook his head. He would hide from them always. The happy relationship Andrew enjoys with his liberal, accepting parents is probably his most powerful weapon against Nathan, and the one which he withholds until the last minute, for the final attack.

"I'm carrying the alumni group banner in the march this year," Andrew says.

"Good," says Nathan.

"I really wish you'd come. You'd like it. Everyone will be there, and it's a lot of fun to march."

"Drop it, Andrew," Nathan says. "You know how I feel. I think that kind of public display doesn't do any good to anyone. It's ridiculous."

"It does the marchers a lot of good. It does the world a lot of good to see people who aren't ashamed of who they are."

"That's not who *I* am," Nathan says. "Maybe it's part of *what* I am. But not who." He turns and looks at the rose garden outside the window. "Don't you see," he says, "that it's a question of privacy?"

"In any battle for freedom of identity there can be no distinction between the private and the political."

"Oh, great, quote to me from the manual," Nathan says. "That helps. You know what's wrong with your party-line political correctness? Exactly what's wrong with your march. It homogenizes gay people. It doesn't allow for personal difference. It doesn't recognize that maybe for some people what's politically correct is personally impossible, emotionally impossible. And for a politics which is supposed to be in favor of difference, it certainly doesn't allow for much difference among the 'different.' " His pronunciation of this word brings to their minds the voices of elementary school teachers.

"I think you're underselling politics, Nathan," Andrew says.

"Oh, just give me a break, Andrew, give me a break," Nathan says. "You know the only reason you ever found politics was because you had a crush on what's-his-name—Joel Miller—senior year. You had a huge crush on him and you were scared little Andrew and you were afraid to use the word gay. I remember distinctly all the little ways you had of talking around that word. 'I'm joining the widening circle,' was all you could say to Celia. I remember that. 'The widening circle.' Where in hell you came up with that phrase is beyond me. And then there's hunky Joel Miller who'll only sleep with you if you wear a lavender armband and talk about 'pre-Stonewall' and 'post-Stonewall' every chance you get and suddenly our little Andrew is Mr. Big Political Activist. Jesus. You're right about your politics, about there being no separation between the private and the political."

He turns away from Andrew, clearly disgusted, picks up the jacket of the Ravel record and begins to read the liner notes furiously.

"I can't stand this anymore," Celia says, then sits down on the sofa. Neither of them seem to have heard her. Nathan looks as if he might start crying any second—he cries easily—and a slick smile is beginning to emerge on Andrew's face.

"Nathan," he says, "do I detect a note of jealousy in your voice?"

"Go to hell," Nathan says, and storms out of the room.

"That's right, that's right, run away," says Andrew, marching after him to the library door. "Just go cry on Daddy's lap, why don't you, you just go tell him all about it."

"Stop it," Celia says. He turns around, and she is in front of him, her face wrathful. "Jesus Christ," she says, "you two are children. He overreacts to you, and the minute he's vulnerable, you just go for the balls, don't you? You just hit him right where it hurts?"

"Give me a break, Celia," Andrew says. "He's been asking for it, he's been taunting me all weekend. I'm sorry, but I'm not going to be his little punching bag, not anymore. I'm the stronger one. What just happened proves it."

"All it proves is that you can be as cruel to him as he can be to you," Celia says. "Big shit."

"He knows I'm sensitive about dancing, so he goes after me about it. He treats me like a heedless fool whose only purpose in life is to break all his parents' precious possessions. Well, I'm not a fool, Celia, I'm a hell of a lot better put-together person than he is."

"All the more reason why you shouldn't hurt him," Celia says. "You know all that stuff about the march, about his parents, you know what a sore subject that is for him. Not to mention Joel Miller."

"And all that time I was seeing Joel, did he say a word to me? Did he even talk to me? No! That time, Celia, he hurt me more than I could ever possibly have hurt him."

Celia laughs, then—a hard, shrill laugh. "Let's add up points," she says. "Let's see who's been hurt the most."

Nathan and Andrew became lovers in Florence, the summer after junior year. It happened only a few days before their scheduled rendezvous with Celia in Rome. That summer, like every summer, Nathan was a wanderer, a rich boy, one of hordes of backpack-bearing students trying to make the most of their Eurail passes. Andrew was in Europe under more impressive auspices; he had won a fellowship to study the influence of Mannerism on the Baroque, using as his chief example the statuary of several late sixteenth-century Italian gardens. Celia's journey began later and ended earlier than her friends' because she didn't have much money, and had to get back to slave at a secretarial job in order to earn funds for her next year in college. She had never been to Europe before, and when she met her friends in Rome, she was exuberant with stories to tell them about her travels in England and France. In particular she wanted to tell them about a tiny town in Wales which had a wall and a moat, and how—big and uncoordinated as she was—she had climbed to the top of the old stone wall and marched its perimeter, as guard-ian knights had done in the thirteenth century. From the top of the wall, she could see the town—snug houses crammed together, and ruins of a castle, and the bay where fishermen caught salmon at high tide. And there, above it all, was Celia. She felt a rare self-confi-dence, and for once she liked the way she imagined she looked to other people—smart and self-assured, aware of how to travel right, able to drink in the pleasures of Europe without falling prey to its pitfalls and inconveniences. Indeed, arriving in Italy, Celia was so distracted by herself that it took her a few days to figure out what was going on between Nathan and Andrew. She talked and talked, and they sat across from her, their hands in front of them, and listened politely. Then, on the third day of their week together, the two of them insisted on keeping the double room they were sharing, and keeping Celia in an expensive single, even though a cheaper triple had opened up. She wondered why, and knew. That afternoon they walked out to the Catacombs, and on the way they played a game called In My Grandmother's Trunk. "In my grandmother's trunk," Nathan began, "I found an addlepated aardvark." Now it was Andrew's turn. "In my grandmother's trunk," he declaimed, "I found an addlepated aardvark and a bellicose bovine." Celia twisted her hair around her pinky and thought about it. "In my grandmother's trunk, I found an addlepated aardvark, a bellicose bovine, and a crenellated chrysanthemum," she said at last, smiling, proud of her answer. Nathan didn't even look at her, though he had laughed at Andrew's response. She realized they were in love as well as lovers then—recognizing, she supposes now, a certain secretiveness in the way they spoke, the way they listened for each other's answers, as if they were talking in code. They offered each other enervated earwigs and truncated turnips as if they were precious gifts, until the game became something which had no place for Celia. Andrew was not out of the closet, then, and as far as she knew, he and Nathan knew each other only through her. The meeting among the three of them had been arranged spontaneously over one of the dinners the three of them had together. "Let's say, July twenty-fourth, in front of the Pantheon," said Nathan, who knew Rome (he claimed) as well as he knew New York. Andrew and Celia, neither of whom had been to Europe before, both marvelled that it was even possible to plan here, in the New World, for actual rendezvous in the strange Old World of Marcus Aurelius and Isabella Sforza and Eleanora de Toledo. And Nathan, too, enjoyed his status, as expert, as experienced traveller. He would show them everything, he told them. He would be a marvel-lous tour guide. Falling asleep that night, Celia had thought of books she had read as a child in which trios of children went on adventures together in distant lands and on other worlds. But apparently, Nathan and Andrew had made some other plans without telling her, to meet earlier, and alone; apparently they had been seeing each other without her, and without her knowing; apparently, she realized, walking away from Rome, they were no longer hers, but each other's.

Celia finally confronted them over Orzata at a café on the Piazza Navona. "I want you to know that I'm aware of what's going on," she said, "and I think we should talk about it." In fact, Nathan did all the talking, while Andrew wriggled, embarrassed and terrified. What Celia remembers most vividly about that afternoon is the overwhelming desire to bolt and run which took her over. She thought longingly of her town in Wales, and of the old, crumbling wall, and of herself atop it, and she wished she could transport herself back there, just for an instant, and regain—now, when she needed it—that rare feeling of freedom, of having surpassed the needy world.

She congratulated them (and thought, how stupid, as if it's an achievement); said she was happy for them (and thought, why am I so unhappy for myself?); agreed willingly to stay in her single room. But should she stay at all? Wouldn't it be better if she left, and left the two of them alone? No, never! Of course they wanted her, she must stay. So she did. A few days later, they visited the garden of the Villa d'Este at Tivoli. Andrew was doing his research, taking furious notes about certain bas-reliefs of men turning into fishes. Andrew read to Nathan from his notebook:

It is the final act of reclamation that moss is destroying their faces. What's thematized here is an endless battle between nature and art. On one level, nature subjugates the men by turning them into lower forms of life, but really art is subjugating nature. The fishes' mouths are part of the drainage system—a technical wonder in the sixteenth century—which allows the fountain water to ceaselessly recirculate, by means of a number of pumps. Only now is nature taking its revenge, by destroying these fish faces, a little at a time, year after year. Wearing them down, growing them over with moss. Moss and wind and time. How long can Tivoli last?

Triumphantly he closed the blue notebook, which was printed with the insignia of their university. "Well?" he said.

"How poetic," said Nathan.

Andrew looked at him. "What do you mean?" he asked.

"I mean," Nathan said, "it's all lovely and sensitive, but I really can't believe you're making all these claims when you have no basis in historical fact. How can you know that what you say is going on is what was intended?"

"Historical fact," Andrew said, "is the historicist's fiction. I don't pretend I can know anyone's intention. I'm doing a *reading* of the garden."

It went on from there. Andrew accused Nathan of being a pedant, and Nathan accused Andrew of evading the rigors of scholarship. Already Celia understood more about them than they did about themselves: Andrew was impulsive, Nathan cautious; Andrew had a reason to be in Europe, Nathan had none (and was jealous). She found the matter altogether tedious, so she wandered away from them and fell in with a tour group from Oklahoma. The group was standing in front of the statue of Diana of Ephesus, her twelve breasts spouting water into an ancient urn, and the guide was talking about the Goddess being a symbol of natural fertility. "Some say she is related to Vishnu," he said solemnly, "the God with the thirteen hands."

"I'll bet her husband was the guy with the thirteen hands!" a woman with a beehive hairdo bellowed, and everyone roared, and Celia—standing among them—realized suddenly that she, too, was laughing, and that she had to leave.

She went the next morning. At the train station, Nathan and Andrew pleaded with her, begged her to stay, but she was decided. She got on an all-night train to Calais, and a ferry back to England, and another train to London. And after a single night in a hostel in Knightsbridge she took all the money she had left and bought a round-trip ticket to her beloved little town in Wales. Almost as soon as she got there she checked into a bed-and-breakfast and went to look at the old stone wall. There was a group of children no more than nine or ten years old being led around it, children from some industrial town in the Midlands, with Mohawk haircuts and dirty black vinyl jackets on. They were fighting with each other over candy, pretending to push each other off the wall. Then they started yelling things at her—obscenities she could hardly understand—and she hurriedly walked away and stood on the grass of the town green and closed her eyes. The air was fresh with the smell of recent rain, as well as the smell of biscuits baking nearby. An old man sitting on a stone bench hobbled over to her, and started speaking to her, but his Welsh accent was so strong that she thought he was speaking in another language, Finnish or Dutch. "Slower, please, slower," she said, until she finally realized he was asking her why she was crying. "Crying?" she said, and put her hands to her eyes, which were moist with tears.

Across a continent, Nathan and Andrew were not even thinking about her.

Although they've knocked repeatedly on his door, Nathan has apparently resolved not to acknowledge the presence of his friends this afternoon, and so, around three o'clock, Andrew and Celia take a walk to the beach. Celia is determined to spend most of the day outdoors, with or without Nathan. He has brooded too long, and she is losing patience with him. Andrew, on the other hand, cannot stop worrying about his friend; his brief triumph has left in its wake a weighty sense of guilt. "I guess I won," he tells Celia, "and it felt so good. But now I wish I'd lost. I don't like this feeling. You know, he's won practically every argument we've ever had."

"Don't be too upset about him," Celia says. "You know how he is. He broods. Anyway, I thought you were so happy to have put him in his place."

"But that's just it," Andrew says. "I'm not supposed to put him in his place. I'm not supposed to do that."

"Andrew, that's ridiculous," Celia says. "Things change in relationships, and maybe this means you're breaking out of the old pattern."

Andrew shakes his head violently, and pushes a mosquito out of his face. "It just doesn't work that way," he says. "For years I've had this idea of who he was and who I was. I knew I was more politically aware and had a healthier attitude toward sex and toward being gay. And I knew he was politically backward and closeted and conservative and torn apart because the fact that he liked to sleep with men contradicted everything he was raised to be. But all that time, he still had this power over me because he was the first person I slept with. He'll never let go of the fact that I was a scared little boy and he knew exactly what he was doing."

"I'm not so sure that's true," Celia says.

"But he did that for me, Celia. That first night we met in Florence, we were so scared, we both knew what we were there for, why we'd come, but we couldn't even seem to talk about it. Every gesture— every mention of anything having to do with being gay—seemed very courageous, because I still believed, on some level, that he'd be horrified if he found out I wanted to sleep with him, and say something like, 'How could you think I'd want to do that? ' I mean, I really didn't know about Nathan. I was going on instinct. And then, finally, we were both in the room in the *pensione*, and we were sitting on his bed, and he wouldn't do anything. We just sat there, and five minutes went by, and not a word. I couldn't move."

"Why?"

"You see, it was understood that he was more experienced. And that he would make the first move. I can't explain why, but it just was. And then he started coughing. Oh, God, I was scared. And I patted him on the back. And I just didn't move my hand away again.

"He said, 'You're very suave,' and then I hoisted my legs up on the bed—I was sitting and he was lying—and in the middle of getting up on the bed I got this terrible charley horse and started screaming and he just laughed. He bent me over and sort of wrenched my leg into shape again. And then—well, we made love. It was very greedy. No subtlety, no technique. But it was still very definitely 'making love,' not just sex." He laughs. "I remember there were these two drunk Americans who came into the room next to ours late that night from the Red Garter singing 'Superfreak.' And then around three one of them must have had a nightmare because he ran out into the hall and started screaming, and then crying. The other one tried to shut him up, but he just wailed and wailed. I remember exactly what his friend said. He said, 'Hey, man, chill out, don't freak.' Nathan was asleep, and we were wrapped around each other in an incredibly complicated way. I could feel all the hairs on his body, and his breath, and his heartbeat. I lay awake all night."

For several minutes they have been walking by the ocean without realizing it. The beach is almost empty except for a single sunbather, and a woman swimming laterally alongside the shore.

"The next day," Andrew says, "we ran into this girl I knew from my botany class the semester before. Charlotte Mallory, you remember her? We had dinner with her. Nathan had his leg pressed against mine under the table the whole time. It was a wonderful secret, something to look forward to, what we'd try that night, everything I had to learn."

He stops, smiles, and turns to face Celia. "This isn't fair of me, is it?" he says. "Imposing this all on you."

"Oh, don't start on that," Celia says. "Andrew, I just wonder why you and Nathan feel you have to keep this thing up. I mean, sure, it was nice once, but it always turns out like it did today. You two know too well how to hurt each other. The memory's precious, but look what it's given rise to, look at yourselves now."

They are walking again, away from the beach, back toward Nathan's parents' house. Andrew has his hands in his pockets, and keeps his eyes on the ground in front of him. "Celia," he says, "there's something you've got to understand about me and Nathan. He taught me things."

"Taught you what?"

"Growing up a fag is a strange thing. You never learn about boys' bodies because you're afraid of what you will feel and you never learn about girls' bodies because you're afraid of what you won't feel. And so the first time you sleep with someone, it's like the first time you've ever noticed a body. I watched everything. I remember I was amazed to see the way his diaphragm moved up and down when he slept because I'd never watched anyone sleep before. And for showing me that, because of that, I'll always love him, even if he acts the way he does. I'll never forget the way he looked, sleeping."

They keep walking. Celia doesn't say anything.

"It's because of that," Andrew says, after a few seconds, "that he'll always have an advantage on me. You know what I was just remembering? How that whole summer we stayed in *pensiones*, and usually there were two single beds in the rooms we were given. And in the morning, Nathan always insisted we unmake the bed we hadn't slept in. And I always assumed, and he always assumed, that the unslept-in bed was mine."

They are in the garden now. Celia looks at the tilled earth beneath her feet, raw end-of-season, everything picked. No sign of Nathan.

"Oh, Celia," Andrew says, "this is mean of me."

"What?"

"It's cruel of me. It must make you feel like you aren't a part of it. But you are. You're very dear to us both."

"You sound like I'm your adopted child," Celia says.

"I'm sorry. I don't mean to. It's just—well, I think you should know. Nathan's always thought you were in love with him on some level, and that's why you've stuck around with us."

Celia looks up at him, startled, and her eyes narrow. She tells herself that she knows what he is doing. He is trying to get her on his side. Nothing unusual. Even so, the revelation, which is no revelation at all, hits her hard, in the stomach.

She looks away from him. "Why I've stuck around with you?" she says. "I've stuck around with you because I love you both. I'm devoted to you both. But if Nathan thinks I've just been panting after him all these years, he's flattering himself."

Andrew laughs, and she curses the slight timbre of resentment in her voice. She does not want to satisfy him by seeming recriminating. Yet she is thinking, why, after all? And she thinks, has it finally arrived, the day when she must confront herself? It has almost arrived many times, and there has always been a reprieve.

"He's just an egotist, I guess," Andrew says. "I mean, he thinks of himself as being like those thousand-dollar speakers of his parents. You have to be so careful around him, though God knows he's willing to hurt everyone else." He smiles affectionately. "Poor Nathan," he says. "You know where he is now? He's in his parents' bedroom, all curled up like a little kid, and he's just lying there, on that huge bed. That's where he goes when he feels small; somewhere where he is small."

They are at the front door now. Andrew turns and looks down at Celia, and suddenly he seems much taller than he did an hour ago. "Would you mind terribly if I went in to him for a little while?" he asks. "Just lie there with him? You can wait in the library, or by the pool. We'll all be ready to leave on the six forty-five."

Celia wraps her arms around her chest "Sure," she says. "Fine." She does not look at Andrew, but at the maple trees, the vines twining up the sides of the house, the fragrant bunches of wisteria.

"I'll see you soon, then," Andrew says. Then there is the sound of his footsteps, the sound of the screen door as it slaps the house.

It is, Celia realizes, a kind of reprieve to be forgotten.

One night, late in the spring of senior year when they were both drunk on big, deceptive rum-and-fruit concoctions, Nathan told Celia the story of the first time he and Andrew slept together. He told it more cheerfully, and he did not mention the unused bed, though he dwelled with loving attention on the painful conversations they had had that night at dinner. "Our feet touched once," Nathan said, "and we both sort of jumped, as if we had given each other an electric shock. The second time our feet touched we just sort of left them there. I kept thinking, If he says anything, I could just say I thought I was resting my foot against a part of the table." And of course, Nathan wasn't asleep either. He remembered the boys next door singing "Superfreak," and the exact words with which the one comforted the other: "Hey, man, chill out, don't freak."

"The thing was," Nathan said, "I had Andrew convinced that I was Mr. Suave, very experienced. And it's true, I was more experienced than he was, but I was a nervous wreck anyway. I mean, being the seducer is a very different thing from knowing how to be seduced. Anyway, when we were alone in the room, I just decided to be brave. So I walked over to Andrew—he was unbuttoning his shirt—and I said, 'Why don't you let me do that?' He just froze. And then I kissed him."

He smiled. Celia knew better than to believe his version, recognizing even then that there were situations in which Nathan had to change the truth, to fit an image of himself which was just a bit wrong, a size too small or too large. After all, Andrew's affair with Joel Miller was at its apex. Nathan was terribly jealous, and it was important to him to prove himself to Celia, since she provided the only link between them. All that year Celia had been insisting that she wanted time to herself, time to pursue her own social life, but almost from the first day Andrew and Nathan wouldn't leave her alone. They wanted her to take sides in the fight they were having. The argument she had witnessed at the Villa d'Este, it seemed, had continued and festered after she left them. They bickered and lashed out at each other until finally, in Paris, Andrew packed his backpack in a fury and, in the middle of the night, stormed out of their little room in the Latin Quarter and boarded a train for Salzburg. By the time he arrived his anger had cooled, and he got on another train back to Paris, but when he got back to their *auberge*, Nathan had checked out and left no forwarding address.

Andrew was seized with panic, for now he was alone, absolutely alone, and there was no way he could find Nathan unless they happened upon each other by chance. Their itinerary was vague, but they had more or less planned to go to Cannes, so Andrew went there, and for two days walked the town tirelessly, scanning the streets and beaches for Nathan, planning what he'd say when he saw him, how aloof and distant he'd be and how he'd draw forgiveness from him. He found it hard to sleep alone again, and he couldn't get out of his nostrils that clean smell of soap and cologne and Nathan. But he never found Nathan in Cannes, or anywhere else in Europe. He continued travelling. By the time he got back to the States, his longing had hardened into something like hatred. And Nathan was angry, too. It was hard to say, after all, who had abandoned whom first, who was to blame for what had happened.

At school they could hardly talk to each other, and so they talked to Celia instead, each giving her his version of what happened in Paris, and trying to win her over to his side. It was the only time, Celia reflected, that two men were rivals for her affections.

She told herself that her position was difficult. At first she had to make sure that Nathan never saw her with Andrew, or vice versa; they insisted on pumping her for information about one another. Then she began to arrange accidental meetings between them; they couldn't help but talk to each other—silence would have seemed too stilted a response, and they both prided themselves on their originality. Finally Andrew called Celia at three o'clock one morning, in tears; she couldn't understand what he was saying, but she managed to get him to tell her where he was, and she put on her coat and trudged out after him. It was just beginning to feel wintry out, and the sky was fringed with blue, as if it were dawn or dusk, and not the middle of the night; and since it was Sunday morning, and just after midterms, there were a few drunk football players still out, tromping around and causing trouble. Celia found Andrew sitting on the post of an old fence, wrapped in a coat he had bought at the Salvation Army, inert. She walked him back to her room, brewed some tea, and sat down in front of him, settling her still-gloved hands comfortably on his knees.

"Now," she said, "what's wrong?"

He started crying almost immediately; she let him cry, hugging him, until his body shivered and his teeth chattered, and, stuttering, he said exactly what she expected him to say: "He doesn't want me. And I love him."

Celia tracked Nathan down the next day, in the library. As soon as she mentioned Andrew's name, he shushed her, and pointed to his roommate—a tall young man smoking a pipe a few feet away—and hurried her off to a nearby cubicle. There he explained that he had had absolutely enough of Andrew's impulsiveness and silliness. To first simply run away in the middle of the night, stranding Nathan in Paris, and now, after two months, to show up suddenly in his room— thank God his roommate hadn't been home!—and start blubbering about not wanting to keep up the charade, about wanting to talk, about feeling hurt and intimidated by Nathan's behavior toward him in Paris. All of this, naturally, was too much, considering it was Andrew who had all but abandoned Nathan, and to cap it off, he had to be loud about it. So Nathan told him to get out, it was over, he was making a mountain out of a molehill. Of course, even then, sitting in the library cubicle, Celia knew better than to take Nathan's version of things at face value. She realized Nathan was angry, but also, that he was fright- ened by Andrew's willingness to make a passionate display over matters Nathan felt best left in the bedroom. Where Nathan's skill lay in small, private insults, Andrew's great tactic was, and would always be, display. Probably Nathan realized that his friend was, as Celia would put it, about to shoot out of the closet like a cannonball, and this was more than his ingrained sense of propriety would allow him to accept. Fear lay behind that sense of propriety. Little Andrew, for all his innocence, was turning out to be the one thing Nathan never could be: He was turning out to be brave. So Nathan chose not to forgive Andrew his actions in Paris, and dropped him.

Shortly thereafter, people started seeing Andrew in the company of the famous activist, Joel Miller, and the rest was fairly predictable. Joel Miller had done it before, with other apparently uncorruptible young men, and they always emerged from the affairs card-carrying members of the lavender left. Ostensibly, Nathan shouldn't have cared, but Celia could see what was in his eyes when he spied Andrew and Joel eating together in a dining hall. Nathan couldn't stay silent very long about it. "What's he doing spending so much time with that Joel Miller person?" he'd say to Celia, figuring she'd leak information, but Celia made it a new policy not to talk about Andrew with Nathan, or vice versa. Soon the affair became a public phenomenon, and Nathan's discomfort increased. He slunk away whenever he saw them, and usually left the parties they attended together. ("They walk into the room like they're the football captain and the homecoming queen," he'd tell Celia.) As for Andrew, he was in bliss; Joel was a genius; he wanted to marry Joel. Celia could afford to be happy for him, because she had her hands full taking care of Nathan, who showed up at her door at all hours. She pitied Nathan; he could never admit that he was terribly intimidated by Joel Miller, or that he might have loved Andrew. Still, she had him. He was there all the time—at her door, waiting for her in the dining hall, in the library. She controlled what he and Andrew heard about one another, and she, of course, knew everything about both of them. One night she would listen to Nathan's anxieties, his claims to misery and loneliness; the next night, to Andrew's praises of the wonders of love, the transcendence of gender roles, and the lovely, dark hair which curled over Joel Miller's shoulder blades.

It did not occur to Celia until a long time later—when she was able to gain some perspective on that year, in which things had been the most intense between them—that her happiness with Nathan and

Andrew depended on Nathan and Andrew being unhappy with each other.

Around dusk, Nathan and Andrew emerge from the house. They are dressed in different clothes from the ones they were wearing earlier, and they are talking animatedly, eagerly, occasionally laughing. As soon as she sees them, Celia closes her eyes. She is lying by the pool, the copy of *Army Slave* open on her lap, and all around her fireflies are exploding with light, crickets screeching. "Come on, Celia, get ready to go," Nathan says. She opens her eyes and he is leaning over her, smiling. "My parents may be back any second, and I don't want to be here when they arrive." He pats her knee, and heads back to the patio, where Andrew is waiting. "Oh," he says, turning around, "and don't forget to bring the magazine." She lifts up her head, but in the dusk light, she can just barely make out their faces. "I guess you're feeling better," she says.

"Yes," Nathan says. "Much better."

She nods, and gets up to pack her things. It is about a ten-minute walk to the train station, and when they get there, the platform is already full of tired-looking people in shorts, all yawning and opening up their newspapers. When the train pulls in, it's already crowded; there are no sets of three seats together. Andrew sits with Celia, and Nathan sits alone, two rows behind them, but the arrangement is entirely for her benefit. Something has happened between Nathan and Andrew this afternoon: They appear to have forgiven each other. Why else would they be thinking about her?

She lies back, watches the pleasurable journey from the scum of Penn Station to the beautiful Hamptons run backward; now they are in the famous suburbs of the Guyland (as Nathan calls it), now in the nether regions of Queens. When they pass the exact border between

New York City and the rest of the world, Nathan cannot resist walking up to point it out to them.

Then they are in the tunnel under the East River, and under the famous city where they spend their lives.

They get off the train. Penn Station has no air-conditioning, and is packed with people. Celia wipes the sweat off her brow, and rearranges her bags between her legs. She will take the Broadway local to the Upper West Side, while Nathan and Andrew must walk across town to catch the East Side subway, and ostensibly ride it in opposite directions. She has no doubt but that they will spend tonight, and perhaps tomorrow night, together; and she wonders if they will eat dinner out, see a movie, talk about her, and shake their heads. It will last a few days; then, she is confident, they will fight. One of them will call her, or both of them will call her. Or perhaps they will decide to move in together, and never call her again.

"I've got to catch my train," Celia says, when it becomes clear that they're not going to invite her out with them. She offers them each her cheek to kiss as if to give them her blessing. They look at her a little awkwardly, a little guiltily, and she can't believe they're acting guilty now, when it's been like this for so many years between them. Besides, there really isn't anything anyone can apologize for. Celia begins to walk away, and Nathan calls out her name. She turns, and he is next to her, a big smile plastered on his face. "You know," he says, "you're wonderful. When I write my book, I'm dedicating it to you."

She smiles back, and laughs. He said the same thing the day she left them at Termini station in Rome and boarded a train for Calais. All that night the couchette car in which she slept was added on and taken off of other strings of lit cars, passed among the major trains and in this way, like a changeling infant, carried singly to the coast. She shared a cabin with two Englishwomen on their way back from holiday and a Swiss man who was going to Liverpool to buy a spare part for his car. Like college roommates, the four of them lay in their bunk beds and talked late into the night. The wheels rumbled against the tracks, the train moved on; every minute she was closer to England. Then she fell asleep, wondering to herself what kind of book Nathan could ever possibly write.

A NOTE ON THE AUTHOR

David Leavitt's books include the novels *The Lost Language of Cranes*, *While England Sleeps* (finalist for the Los Angeles Times Fiction Award), *The Body of Jonah Boyd*, *The Indian Clerk* (finalist for the PEN/Faulkner Award and shortlisted for the IMPAC Dublin Literary Award) and *The Two Hotel Francforts*. He is also the author of two nonfiction works, *The Man Who Knew Too Much: Alan Turing and the Invention of the Computer* and *Florence, A Delicate Case*. His writing has appeared in the *New Yorker*, the *New York Times*, the *Washington Post*, *Harper's*, *Vogue*, and *The Paris Review*, among other publications. He lives in Gainesville, Florida, where he is professor of English at the University of Florida and edits the literary magazine *Subtropics*.

DISCOVER THE NOVELS OF DAVID LEAVITT

"One of the major voices of contemporary fiction." —*The Guardian*

The Lost Language of Cranes

"A tour de force." —*The New York Times*
"Brilliant, wise . . . It would be hard to
overpraise this book." —*Vogue*

Trade paperback ISBN: 978-1-62040-702-8
eISBN: 978-1-62040-703-5

The Indian Clerk

"Richly imagined . . . Offers the pleasure
of escape into another world."
—*The New York Times Book Review*
"Ambitious, meaty . . . Refreshingly
original."
—*San Francisco Chronicle*

Paperback ISBN: 978-1-59691-041-6
eISBN: 978-1-59691-840-5

While England Sleeps

"Extraordinary . . . Deeply moving." —*People*
"A sprawling novel of star-crossed lovers . . .
[Leavitt is] an extremely graceful novelist."
—*Los Angeles Times*

Trade paperback ISBN: 978-1-62040-708-0
eISBN: 978-1-62040-701-1

The Two Hotel Francforts

"Crackling with intrigue and illicit
romance."
—*O, the Oprah Magazine*
"Moving, ravishing and fiercely ambitious,
this is a novel to treasure." —*The Guardian*

Paperback ISBN: 978-1-59691-043-0
eISBN: 978-1-60819-599-2

Available now wherever books are sold
www.bloomsbury.com